THE LAST CHANCE

WINTER K. WILLIS

CONNECT WITH WINTER

Winter K. Willis is a pseudonym for our two-person writing team. We like to think of it as our band name. We love telling our character's stories and hope that you enjoy reading them.

For info on our latest releases, sign up for our newsletter at www.winterkwillis.com

Published by Celestial Bear Publishing

ALSO BY WINTER K. WILLIS

THE WIFE INSIDE

HOW THE AFFAIR ENDS

BEHIND THE NEIGHBOR'S DOOR

THE PERFECT GIFT

THE PERFECT EX-WIFE

THE ASSISTANT

PROLOGUE - MILES

BY WINTER K. WILLIS

My heart races, every beat echoing the urgency of my pace as I walk through the resort's dimly lit halls. Earlier that evening, Kora's music filled the banquet hall as we celebrated the resort's opening. Now, a heavy, haunting quiet has settled over me and the only sounds are our shoes thudding against the polished floors and ragged breaths I can't seem to control.

Sarah, our seasoned lead cook and I approach Kora's door and knock, but there is no answer. After several attempts, my fingers, ice-cold from dread, hesitantly wrap around the doorknob. I inhale deeply, trying to steady myself to prepare for whatever lies beyond that door.

I turn the lights on and see Kora laid out on the carpet in the middle of the floor. Her curly hair is sprawled around her. I walk over to her; Sarah trails behind me.

I lean closer to her. Her light-brown skin is drained of its warmth. "Kora. Kora, wake up," I say.

Kora doesn't move.

I kneel beside her and place a hand on her shoulder. "Hey. Hey Kora."

She feels cold and rigid.

My heart quickens. I check her pulse.

"Wait, is she. . ." Sarah starts.

I place my face next to her nose and mouth, searching for any signs of breath or life, but there are none. I look up at Sarah. "Yeah, I think she's..." I start. I can't bring myself to finish the sentence.

"C.P.R. We should do C.P.R." says Sarah.

"She's already cold," I say. But I immediately start compressions anyway. In between the compressions, I breathe air into her body, but I know it's too late.

I tire and stop. Sarah is shaking. I fight to keep my composure. I can tell that Sarah is about to lose it. We can't have both of us incapacitated; we need to figure out what happened.

Kora's usually radiant face, now cold and still, is a stark contrast to the glamorous sequined dress she wore for her performance earlier this evening. In normal circumstances, this resort guest room should have been a place of solitude for her, but instead, it has become a tomb. I try to push the grim thought out of my mind and resume compressions. I know it's already too late, but I have to try something. Anything to keep from falling apart.

Nearby, Sarah stands like a statue, her robust frame paralyzed by shock. Her apron, stained with sauces and spices, seems out of place in this grim setting. Sarah shouldn't even be here right now. I dragged her from her middle-of-the-night prep to come with me to check on Kora. I know I have to get help, but I can't leave Sarah here alone.

I stand in front of her. "Sarah, run to the desk. The landline should have reception. Call for help."

Sarah's eyes water up, but she doesn't fully let herself fall into despair. "What happened to her?" She asks.

"Sarah, go get help," I repeat.

Sarah nods frantically and runs out of the room.

I take a deep breath and run through what I know in my mind. Kora and I agreed to meet right after the show last night, just behind the stage. Shortly after the show ended, I made my way behind the screen to wait for her, but minutes turned to ten minutes and then eventually an hour. It's not like Kora to keep people waiting, so I naturally began to worry that something had gone terribly wrong. When I thought she was ignoring my texts, I tried to take the hint. When I heard whispers among the staff that something happened during her performance, I knew I had to check in on her. I was too late.

Dragging my eyes away from the heart-wrenching scene, I scan the room, searching desperately for some clue, some hint of what might have transpired.

She is so healthy. She was, I think. If she wasn't sick, was it drugs or something? I rule it out, remembering that she rarely drank on special occasions. Then a whisper of a thought begins to form in the back of my mind. What if someone did this to her? I don't even know how to tell.

I stand in silence, looking around the room. There are no overt signs of a struggle. If a killer was here, they vanished, leaving nothing behind. It almost looks like she laid herself down. No furniture is disturbed around her. Wouldn't there be something off if someone killed her and she fell? Maybe it was some sort of freak medical emergency.

I don't know what to look for; I'm not an expert at this stuff. If there is a killer, why? Why Kora? I step to the doorway of the room before angry tears begin to fall. I feel like all the wind has been taken out of me. The love of my life is gone.

1

AMELIA

Even though I'm in a rush, I take my time going down the stairs of our Las Vegas mid-century farmhouse. The stairs are the only thing I hate about this place. I have at least one dream per week that I will fall head first to the bottom and no one will save me in time.

Garret and I bought this house when we were first married and I've spent the last several years lovingly redecorating and remodeling the entire thing. When we first moved in, the wallpaper was peeling and there were gouges in the plaster that made it look like the previous owners had taken a sledgehammer to the walls. Now, the house is warm and inviting. I love living here, especially knowing it's a home I created for the family I still hope we'll have one day.

When I get to the kitchen, I immediately pull the chicken potpie out of the oven. It's Garret's favorite. Things between Garret and me haven't been right for months, but I know when he bites this, he'll say, "Amelia, you've outdone yourself." At least I hope so.

We used to be so happy. Garret has always worked long

hours as a corporate salesperson and I've gotten used to that. It's normal for him to work until nine or ten o'clock at night. But things have been worse since he started his own company; now, I almost never see him. Even when he worked late, he always made sure to be home for dinner, even if he had to go back to work after. That hour between six and seven was sacred for us — a time to reconnect. Lately, though, he's been finding excuses to skip it too.

Thirty minutes pass. I glance at my phone. No missed calls, no messages. I open the messaging app and quickly type, *where are you* and hit send.

I make my way to our room, checking my phone again. Nothing. He can't even be bothered to respond to a simple message. What happened to us? How did we drift so far apart? It feels like we're strangers living under the same roof.

I look in the bathroom mirror, ready to give myself a pep talk on not being pathetic, but I look exhausted. Dark bags sit heavy under my eyes and my mousy brown hair is pulled back in a messy bun. I glance down at my shirt, which is dusted with flour — a remnant of my attempt at homemade pie crust.

I'm a hot mess. No wonder Garret doesn't want to come home to this. I used to always be so put together. How did I end up here? I need to do something to reignite the spark between us — remind Garret of what we used to be. I'm afraid that if I don't, our marriage will be over.

To make everything perfect, I clean the kitchen, take a quick shower and throw on a nightgown. A few more hours pass and I'm defeated. I can't keep doing this. I resign and slip under the bed covers when I hear the garage door open. Garret's finally home. My heart pounds as anxiety knots in my stomach, making my hands clammy. A few moments later, he walks into the room, yanking his tie off from around his neck.

"You're late," I say quietly. I want to scream at myself for not being more assertive.

He doesn't answer, just continues undressing. Even after all these years of ups and downs, I'm struck by how handsome he still is. He's managed to stay fit with his daily runs and his sandy blond hair is still perfectly styled. I think about the reflection I saw in the mirror earlier and shake my head. He hasn't changed much, but I've changed so much. Maybe if I could go back to being the person I was, things between us would be different.

"Garret, can we talk?" I ask as he slips into a pair of shorts and a T-shirt.

He hesitates, then shrugs. "Okay. What do you want to talk about?" He walks into the adjacent bathroom, opens the vanity, grabs his painkillers and swallows one with a sip of water straight from the faucet. When he returns, he crawls into bed beside me.

"Is your shoulder bothering you again?" I ask.

He rolls his eyes. "That's not what you really want to talk about."

He's right, so I let it go. Turning toward him, I cross my legs under the blanket and try to meet his eyes. "Garret, I'm worried about us."

"Worried?" He frowns.

"We barely talk anymore. And lately, you don't even come home for dinner. I'm scared we're drifting apart."

"You know how demanding my job is, Amelia. I'm not an employee — I can't just clock in and out. If I don't put in the hours, the business doesn't survive."

Why does he always have to be so dramatic about it? I'm only asking for one hour a day. Just one hour.

I sigh. "I know you work hard, Garret, but if we don't make time for us, we're not going to make it. I'm starting to wonder if you even want to be married anymore."

His eyes snap to mine. "What? Why would you think that?"

"Because you're not present. Not emotionally, not physically. What's the point of being married if we never even talk?"

He leans back against the pillows, exasperated. "What do you want to talk about, Amelia? Let's talk now."

"That's not what I mean. I don't have something specific in mind. I just want us to spend time together."

"You know this is just a phase. Once the business is fully running and I have employees to take over some of the work, things will change. I just need more time."

"This business has been open for five years, Garret. If things haven't changed by now, when will they?"

His jaw tightens. "What are you trying to say? I don't criticize you about your work."

I shake my head, frustrated. He loves to bring up the fact that I work for a chain grocery store as if it is so bad. People all over the country love our little specialty stores, our specialty items and our personable customer service. I don't always feel jolly like our corporate image, but I refuse to feel embarrassed for working there. This conversation is spiraling out of control.

I take a breath and continue. "I'm not trying to say anything. I just want to spend time with you. Our anniversary is coming up next month."

"I know," he mutters.

"Well, I found this new resort in Utah, somewhere in the Rockies. They're having an opening weekend event. I thought we could go — just the two of us, like we used to.

It's all-inclusive: food, entertainment, everything. What do you think?"

"We've got everything right here in Vegas. Why not just go to dinner on The Strip?"

"Come on, Garret."

He runs a hand through his perfectly styled hair. "I don't know, Amelia."

"We used to do the most amazing things for our anniversary. Remember Hawaii? Or the Dominican Republic?"

"Of course, I remember," he says, annoyed.

"In those early years, we went everywhere. We had so much fun together. I miss that, Garret. I miss us."

He doesn't respond right away. The silence between us feels like a weight pressing down on my chest, making it hard to breathe.

"What's the point?" he finally says, his voice tinged with bitterness. "Do you really think a weekend away will fix everything?"

His words cut deep, slashing at the fragile hope I've been holding onto. "I'm not expecting miracles, Garret. I just... I just want to find some piece of what we used to have. Isn't that worth trying for?"

He shifts slightly, glancing at me. After a few agonizing seconds, his shoulders slump. "All right, Amelia," he says quietly. "If this is what you want, we'll go."

Relief washes over me. I reach for his hand, clasping it in mine. He doesn't pull away, but he doesn't squeeze back either. "Thank you," I whisper, my throat tight with emotion. "This means everything to me."

Garret nods, his attempt at a smile falling flat. "We'll see," he murmurs. "We'll see."

2

AMELIA

Big snowflakes fall from the sky almost as soon as our plane lands. We grab our bags, walk to the passenger pickup area and look for the van that's supposed to take us up the mountain. I'm excited and hopeful. This is our chance to make a new start. I look at Garret; he's grumpy, as usual, but I won't let his attitude dampen my good spirits.

Garret moves his arm in a giant circle, grimacing at the pain. "I think the altitude and the weather are going to make my shoulder hurt worse than normal."

"Did you bring your painkillers?" I ask.

He nods. "I brought the new prescription I got from the doctor last week. They're supposed to be a little stronger than the last ones, so maybe I won't have to use them as often."

"Hopefully, they work; the last thing I need is a grumpy husband on our anniversary trip," I tease.

"Who are you calling grumpy," he says, giving me a hint of a smile.

Maybe this is actually going to work, I muse.

A fifteen-passenger van picks us up from the airport. Garret and I are standing at the curb waiting for our ride when the van pulls up.

"Mr. and Mrs. Lawson?" The driver asks.

I look at Garret and then back at the van; this is definitely not what I had expected.

"Yes," I acknowledge hesitantly. "That's us."

Garret has a scowl on his face. I can't remember the last time we took public transportation.

The driver hops out of the van, grabs our bags and tosses them in the back of the van. I climb in first to see two other couples already seated. I slide into the first row, nestling myself against the window. Garret comes in and sits next to me, immediately crossing his arms. "Sorry, Garret. I didn't realize this was a group ride," I whisper.

He turns to me and glares. "This is great, a real awesome start," he says sarcastically.

I turn towards the window and stare outside. I hope this is not an omen for how the entire weekend is going to go.

The drive to the resort is peaceful. At first, the ground is covered in just a light dusting of snow, so light that I can still see the rocks and the trees underneath, but as we climb, the depth of the snow continues to grow. By the time we reach the resort, the entire world is blanketed in white as far as the eye can see and there's no hint of the greens and browns hidden underneath.

"Wow, it's beautiful," I say.

Garret seems to have lost some of his edge. "It is," he responds. "It's been a while since I've seen the snow."

"Remember that one time we went to Breckenridge? And I tried to learn how to ski?"

He chuckles. "Yeah, the Colorado trip was a disaster."

"I fell down that bunny slope at least one hundred times,

but I also remember it being beautiful and cold. But mostly beautiful."

"That was a crazy trip," he says.

Hope springs into me. Maybe if I can just get him to remember all the good times we've had together, we can come back to us — to the way we used to be.

The van exits the freeway and pulls onto what I assume is a dirt road, but it is also covered in several inches of snow. There are no other sounds besides those of the snow and gravel crunching under the tires. The conversation amongst the couples in the van has also stopped as we all look out the windows in anticipation of seeing the newly created resort.

We drive for what seems like forever when suddenly, I see a clearing in front of us and a large structure looming over the horizon.

The closer we get, the more confused I get. "Is that the resort?" I whisper to Garret.

"I'm not sure," he says. "You're the one who booked it."

"It looks like a prison," I say quietly.

The woman behind me exclaims, "oh my gosh, you're right. It does look like a prison. Anyone else think that's kind of creepy?"

A guy in the very back of the van pipes up. "That's because it *was* a prison. That's one of the reasons we came here. We're into horror and the paranormal and this just kinda seemed like the perfect location for ghosts to haunt. Apparently, the cells have been converted to rooms and they've kept some of the aesthetics as part of its charm."

"What's charming about a prison?" I ask.

"I'm not so sure about this," Garret says.

"I'm so sorry, Garret. I had no idea it was going to be like this."

"Seems to me like you didn't do your due diligence. I'm not sure why I trusted you with this."

His words cut me like a knife. I should have been more careful, but I was so excited I didn't question a lot of the details.

He continues. "Well, we're here," he sighs. "I guess we make the most of it. It's not like we can just leave anytime we want. I told you we should have gotten a rental car."

I look out the window and cross my arms. Garret wanted to rent a car for this trip, but I had convinced him to take the shuttle to the resort because it was free. I wish I'd never made the suggestion. If I'd just listened to him, we would at least have a vehicle to get out of here if we needed to, but instead, we're at the mercy of the resort. Maybe if it goes bad, we can ask the staff for a ride back.

The closer we get, the more ominous it feels. At least they removed the barbed wire fence, so there's no feeling of being trapped within the confines of the campus. The resort is a cluster of buildings in the middle of a field, all made with grey concrete slabs. They made no effort to paint it or change it in any way. It still looks like a prison.

The driver pulls up to the front door, gets out and begins to unload our bags. "I will bring in your things. Please follow the signs to the main lobby. I will be with you shortly."

All of us look at each other uneasily, uncertain if we want to get out.

The guy in the back speaks first. "Come on, it'll be an adventure. How many of you ever thought you'd be able to say that you stayed the night in prison?"

We all laugh nervously.

"Alright, fine," Garret says. He grabs the door handle, opens the door and climbs out of the van. I follow right behind him. The air is cold and I wrap my arms around me as if they will provide me extra warmth. It's a good thing I packed warmer coats in our suitcases.

We follow the signs for the lobby and enter the building. It is what I would guess used to be the prison's visiting room. It's a large open space with windows flanking two of the walls. At least they've attempted to make it more upscale and comfortable than the outside. There's artwork on the walls and rugs on the floors. Several Victorian couches are arranged in groups throughout the room. On the far side is a desk with several attendants standing behind, smiling and waiting for us.

I look at Garret nervously. Everything just feels weird and out of place. I could kick myself for not investigating this location further. The virtual flyer showed a few pictures of the rooms and everything looked normal. I didn't bother reading the fine print. How could I expect a refurbished prison? I had no idea what I was getting us into.

3

AMELIA

Garret and I stand in line behind two other couples waiting to check in at the front desk.

"What have you gotten us into, Amelia?" Garret whispers.

"I didn't know it was going to be like this. I would have never booked it if I had known," I reply.

"What kind of research did you do? This wouldn't be hard to figure out." He shakes his head and crosses his arms, clearly pissed. "I don't know how we're supposed to relax in a place like this, let alone reconnect with each other like you want us to. I'm never going to be comfortable."

"Come on, Garret. It's not that bad."

"Did you see the place when we drove in? I've pretty much made it my life's mission to never set foot in one of these places, yet you bring us here on vacation?"

"Maybe just try to see it as an adventure," I suggest, although deep down, I kind of feel the same way. I've made a mess of things.

"Some adventure," he says. "Do you miss your prison

life? Come to our resort and you will feel at home again. That should be their slogan," he adds.

"Well, there's not much we can do about it now except try to make the best of things."

Garret grunts, but says no more.

Ten minutes later, we're at the front of the line. We're greeted by an overly friendly, smiling man in a suit and tie who looks incredibly professional.

"Welcome to The Last Chance Resort," he says, smiling. "My name is Miles. I will be your host this weekend. What are your names?"

"Garret and Amelia Lawson," I say hesitantly.

Garret leans against the counter, his tone laced with sarcasm. "So, Miles, how many prison cells are available? I hear this place used to be a real slammer."

I groan inwardly at his horrible joke.

Miles maintains his composure, his professionalism unwavering. "Yes, it has an interesting history," he responds; his voice is calm and his smile never falters. "The owners thought it would be a unique experience for our guests. Believe it or not, there are quite a few people who love the idea of being able to stay in prison without having to be convicted of something. It's an experience they never dreamed they would be able to have," he says.

"Can't those weirdos just do an escape room or something?" Garret says.

"I've never thought of it that way," says Miles.

"I just think it's ridiculous," Garret continues. "You could have at least painted the outside or something, made it more welcoming."

"The owner wanted to keep it authentic so that our guests could have as close to the real experience as feasible and still maintain a standard of luxury. It's a fine balance."

Garret crosses his arms and looks around him.

Miles smiles. "I see you're staying here for our entire opening weekend."

I nod. "We purchased the grand opening special."

"Wonderful. We have so many fun things planned for our guests this weekend. There will be live entertainment while renowned world chefs serve each meal. I promise you won't be disappointed. Our accommodations might have been a prison, but our amenities are world-class. It's the juxtaposition between the two that people love about us. I think it just might grow on you."

I look around nervously. I hope so. I hope Garret gets over whatever attitude he has about this place so that we can reconnect. That's the whole point of us being here: to give us another chance, but if he can't relax, that's never going to happen.

Miles grabs a white plastic card and inserts it into a machine on the desk. He then types in our room number, followed by the pound sign. "Here's one key," he says, handing the white card to me.

"Thank you," I say.

He then repeats the process and hands the other card to Garret. Once we have the cards, Miles walks over to a pile of bags that I somehow didn't notice before and counts them.

"I have four bags for you, is that correct?"

Alarm bells ring in my mind. "Only four? There's supposed to be five."

Miles moves the bags around to double-check that one is not hiding underneath and turns back towards us. "I'm sorry, but I only see four."

Garret's irritation boils over, his voice sharp. "One of our bags is missing? Are you guys seriously that incompetent?"

Miles's expression remains composed as he reassures us.

"I apologize for the inconvenience. We'll do our best to locate the bag promptly. Rest assured, we'll figure it out."

"Even if you do find it, how do I know the bags are going to remain secure in our room?"

"Excuse me?" Miles asks, confused.

"That whole key card process is one of the most unsecure things I've ever witnessed," he says, gesturing towards the front desk. "Anyone could go back there and do that."

"I appreciate your concern, but it's company policy to have someone behind the desk at all times, so that would be impossible."

"Right, like you can really ensure that's going to happen."

"Garret, leave them alone. This is opening weekend; they're still working out all the kinks and doing the best they can."

"Fine," he grumbles. "But they better find my bag."

Suddenly, movement catches the corner of my eye and takes Garret's full attention. A tall, beautiful, brunette woman walks quickly through the front door and toward the hallway. Her curls are pulled into a French twist, with several tendrils escaping around her face. The woman's radiant, light-brown skin is a stark contrast to the white down jacket that reaches to her ankles. She has a picture ID card hanging around her neck that indicates she's employed by the company and not a guest.

Garret's face turns pale and his previous anger seems to dissipate. He composes himself quickly and turns to Miles. "I'm sure you'll figure out the bag situation," he says.

"Yes, sir. I will send our driver to look for it as soon as I show you to your room."

Garret turns to me. "I'll be right back. I'm gonna look for a restroom."

Before I can even respond that there's probably a restroom in our room, Garret takes off down the same hallway that the woman went down. My face turns bright red with embarrassment.

"I'm so sorry. It looks like you will only be escorting me to our room," I say to Miles.

"No problem," he says. "As soon as your husband gets back, I will make sure he knows how to find you."

A barrage of emotions fills me, but mainly anger at Garret for his inability to just be happy in the moment. I know this is not what we expected, but it really could be a fun adventure if he would just let go.

I'm also confused about where he went. He said he was going to the restroom, but how can I believe that when he suddenly decided he had to go once that woman showed up? Seriously? Why would he follow her right in front of me? It makes no sense.

I take a deep breath to steady and center myself and then nod at Miles. "I'm ready. Let's go."

"Right this way," he says.

He leads me towards a corridor on the opposite side of the room from the one that Garret went down. Before entering the hallway, I turn around one last time to see if he has returned, but there's no sign of him. It's becoming clear that this weekend is not going to turn out as I had hoped.

4

AMELIA

We walk down a dimly lit hallway. It's obvious that the owner has made no attempt to upgrade this part of the former prison. The sound of my heels clicking on the floor is ominous. I can't help but imagine what it would have been like to be walking down this corridor towards my prison cell for the first time. It's a little creepy.

Seconds after entering the hallway, the sound of a rolling cart echoes behind us. I turn and look to see our bags piled on a cart and being pushed by the driver of the van. I smile at him, grateful that he's taken care of our things. I wonder if he's found our lost bag.

Miles opens the door and leads me into a large, open space that has been turned into a lounge-type area. Several couches form groups. Guests are seated on a few of them, drinking cocktails and conversing with each other. A large, mahogany bar rests at the end of the great room staffed with two bartenders. Soft music plays, filling the cold space with warmth.

"This is where many of our guests choose to hang out

during the day and enjoy each other's company," Miles says. "As you can see, we have first-class amenities."

I nod. "I can see you made some attempt to make the place seem luxurious, but it still looks very institutional."

I look around. The two floors above us look like guest rooms and the doors to the rooms look like the original cell doors from the prison.

Miles nods. "The rooms themselves are several cells combined and are very high-end, but as you can see, we left the original doors and some of the bars to keep the prison aesthetic. There are no rooms here on the first floor. We didn't want our guests to be inconvenienced by being so close to the action. We have turned those rooms into other amenities that the guests can take advantage of. On the left side are the restrooms. On the right side is a movie theater that plays a selection of films every evening for the guests to enjoy."

I peek my head in the movie room. Plush recliners are placed in rows in what looks like a multi-room block that has been converted into one big room. At the end of the room is a large screen that fills the entire wall.

I turn back towards Miles. "What floor is our room on?" I ask as I stare up at the two rows of prison cells that have been converted into suites.

"Please, follow me and I'll show you," he says.

We walk towards a small staircase at the end of the room and begin to ascend the steep steps. "You will be on the third floor," he says. "Room five."

I look behind me and see the van driver starting to unload our bags and carry them up the stairs two at a time. I feel a little guilty for packing so much. I didn't realize that it was going to be like this and I'm again grateful for his help.

We get to the top of the stairs and I make the mistake of

looking over the railing. My heart beats a little faster as I stare down at the great room three floors below. I wouldn't say that I'm terrified of heights, but I do avoid them at all costs. I step away from the railing and as close to the wall as I can get, steadying my breath for several seconds.

Miles waits patiently until I'm ready to follow him to room number five. There's a keycard pad on the door, but otherwise, it looks almost how I imagined it did when this building was still used as a prison.

"Wow, they barely even really changed the cell doors," I whisper, amazed. There's a small glass window in the door that is covered by some kind of curtain to allow for privacy. "I guess, at least, it is an actual solid door that closes," I laugh.

"As I said, the owner did his best to maintain the look and feel of the prison while still providing our guests with a world-class experience," Miles says, sounding a tad bit frustrated with having to constantly repeat himself.

The lock on the door clicks and he swings the door open, revealing a very spacious room with no windows.

I gasp. There's a rich, emerald-green carpet underneath the mahogany four-poster bed. Sconces line the walls, casting a dim, romantic vibe throughout the room. At one end of the room is a small bar that looks as though it's fully stocked with every type of alcohol you can imagine.

Miles notices the direction of my gaze. "The bar package is usually an extra fee, but for our opening weekend, the owner has generously placed them in all of the rooms at no additional cost."

"Wow, that is very generous of him," I say. "Will he be here this weekend?"

"No, he didn't want his presence to be a distraction. He is

quite well-known and prefers to remain anonymous when it comes to the operation of this resort."

I nod and continue exploring the room. At the other end of the room, there's a bathroom, but just outside the bathroom is a raised platform with a large hot tub.

"Oh, wow," I exclaim, walking toward the hot tub. "How did you guys even get this up here?"

"We put extra special care into our rooms," Miles says. "We did not want our guests to feel as though they were sleeping in a prison, but in high comfort."

"Well, I think you've done your job. This is lovely." I peek my head inside the gold-trimmed bathroom and am surprised by its size. Not only is there a large, double-headed shower, but there is also a clawfoot tub and two sinks. The attention to detail in this room makes me forget that I'm in a prison; instead, I feel like I'm in a high-class, expensive hotel.

The van driver brings in a load of the bags and then exits to go get the rest.

I look toward Miles. "Out of curiosity, are all the staff housed in this section of the prison as well, or are they somewhere else?" I try to make it sound as though my question is just an afterthought when, in reality, I desperately want to know where Garret could have gone.

"No, the staff are housed in a wing on the opposite side of the campus. The owner renovated the guard's quarters and turned them into staff quarters. The rooms are not nearly as nice as these," he chuckles. "But they are comfortable. I can't complain."

"Well, you're really missing out," I say, hoping my voice sounds light and nonchalant when, in reality, my mind is a swirling vortex of thoughts. Did Garret find the girl he was following? Is he in her room right now? The thought sickens me.

"Please let me know if there is anything else I can do for you," Miles states. "The itinerary for this weekend is printed for you on the bed. Of course, none of the activities that we are hosting are mandatory, but I highly suggest that you not miss them because they are wonderful."

"I think I'm good for now," I say. "Thank you so much for escorting me."

I watch sadly as Miles exits the room and closes the metal door behind him.

The room is quiet and a pang of emptiness settles in my chest. I look around and take in the opulence of the room; its grandeur and warmth contrast with the hollow feeling that I have inside.

My gaze shifts to the hot tub in the corner of the room. The bubbling water looks relaxing and in any other circumstance, I would be tempted to immediately immerse myself in its warmth, but Garret's absence dampens my enthusiasm. I wish he was here and not out there doing who knows what. This was supposed to be our weekend to fix our marriage, but he's already off ruining everything.

I look away from the hot tub and turn my attention to the bar. On top of the bar are several large, full bottles of alcohol of every kind. I consider pouring myself a tall glass of something, anything really. The idea of drowning the emptiness I feel inside is tempting, but I know that numbing the pain won't mend what's broken between us. So what's the point?

I sink onto the edge of the plush bed, my heart heavy with longing and regret. I had hoped to experience seeing this room for the first time together with Garret. I know it's a silly thing, but it's definitely a unique experience to stay in a prison cell and I had hoped that the excitement of experiencing something new together would reignite the passion that has dimmed between us, but he's not even here to enjoy it with me and my hopes for this weekend are slowly dissipating.

I can't give up hope. The weekend is not over and things can still change. I force myself to fill my mind with positive thoughts and I resolutely shake off the melancholy that threatens to consume me, but it's hard to remain optimistic.

As I sit on the bed, the quiet envelops me. How did this start out so poorly? I'm already alone and the weekend hasn't even started. I think about Garret following that woman and emotion overwhelms me. How am I supposed to save my marriage if my husband won't even spend time with me? It's hard not to feel hopeless like I've done all this for nothing.

I take a deep breath and stand. I don't want to spend one more second in this room alone. I need to find Garret.

5

GARRET

My heart races as I speed through the dimly lit hallway, walking as quickly as I can to catch up with the woman. I don't want to yell to get her attention; who knows how loudly my voice will echo in this empty hallway. I just need to catch up to her. Besides, what if I'm wrong? What if she's not who I think she is and I've left my wife to fend for herself for nothing?

I walk as quietly as possible, not wanting to embarrass myself in case I've made a mistake. The woman reaches the end of the impossibly long corridor and turns the corner.

I quicken my pace, determined not to lose sight of her. By the time I get to the end of the hallway and turn the corner myself, she is nowhere to be found.

This corridor is much shorter than the last one and I begin to run, hoping that if I pick up my pace, I'll be able to see which way she turned. There are no doors that she could have disappeared into, so I'm confident that I won't miss her as I run.

When I get to the end of this hallway, I notice that it joins a third hallway in the middle, creating a fork in the road. There are two ways she could have gone. I look to my left and my right and she's nowhere to be found in either direction.

I run my fingers through my hair, not sure which way to choose. The hallways look identical in either direction. I quickly head left. My gut is what told me to go left, but then again, my gut has not always been the most reliable when it comes to making decisions.

I mean, I listened to my gut when I chose to marry Amelia and now look at us. Eleven years in and we're practically strangers. When we got married, I believed with conviction that our love was going to last forever. However, she changed when we started having problems conceiving. I understand that must be hard, but she became almost a shell of the person she used to be.

In the beginning, I tried to give her grace, but days turned into months, which then turned into years and the wife I married never returned.

I know I should have learned to accept her in all stages of our relationship and learned to love the woman she was becoming, but I just couldn't. I threw myself into my work as a way to avoid having to be around her. It sounds awful to me when I think about it. I'm sure that what I'm saying makes me a terrible person, but it's the truth. I guess maybe I never loved her unconditionally like I thought I did.

We probably had no business getting married in the first place, if I'm being honest. If we had just taken more time to get to know each other beyond the honeymoon phase, maybe we would have figured out that we were not right for each other and saved us both some heartache. Instead, I listened to my gut and we got married six months after we met.

I should learn to never listen to my gut.

As soon as I reach the end of the hallway and turn the corner, I'm plunged into near darkness. The lights emanating from the wall sconces only cast a dim glow, making this section of the facility seem ominous. A large sign hangs from the ceiling that says *OFF LIMITS* in bold, red letters. I probably should turn around, but curiosity propels me forward. My original purpose to find the woman is now secondary to my desire to figure out what is in this section of the resort.

There's a large metal door in front of me that has been propped open. I slowly push on it and reveal what looks to be an unrenovated cell block. It's deadly silent in here and the thought of being here alone gives me shivers. I probably shouldn't go inside, but I can't help but want to see what this place looked like before they attempted to turn it into a high-scale hotel.

My footsteps echo in the grand open space. Even though I know the room is no longer full of prisoners, it feels as though I'm being watched by the rows of cells above me.

All the cell doors on the first floor are pulled open. I've never been inside a real prison before. I've seen them on television, but never in real life. It's cold and sterile and I can't imagine what it must be like to spend years in this place.

I peek inside one of the cells and am shocked by its small size. I walk in and reach out, spreading my arms wide. My fingertips graze both walls. The concrete slab that doubles as a bed fills almost the entire room.

In the far corner is a toilet with no toilet seat. I guess they didn't want the prisoners to use the seats to try to escape or hurt someone. On top of the toilet is a sink; it also has no removable parts.

I sink down onto the concrete slab and bury my face in

my hands. How did I end up staying in a prison? What is wrong with Amelia? How could she think this would be even remotely romantic? I sit in silence for several minutes, reflecting on my life. I know Amelia wanted this weekend to be some sort of revival for us, but sitting here in the middle of a prison cell, I highly doubt things are going to change.

I hear a creaking sound coming from outside the cell. I quickly stand and shake my head. I have to get out of here. This place is giving me the willies. I walk into the large open space and hear a loud clanging noise. I rush towards the cell block door, only to find that whatever was propping it open is no longer there. The door is fully shut. I grab the handle and try to turn it, but it's locked.

There are two glass windows in the doors and I stare through them, seeing no one in the hallway. Somebody locked me in here. Why would they do that? How am I going to get out? I tremble as I realize I could be stuck in here for a very, very long time. What have I done?

6

AMELIA

I start my search in the main lobby where I last saw Garret. The lobby is empty now, save for one person standing behind the mahogany desk. I walk towards the corridor Garret went down to follow that woman. It's amazing to me how stupid he thinks I am. He didn't have to go to the bathroom. He just saw a pretty woman and couldn't even help himself. I shake my head. This weekend is the last time I'm going to even attempt to connect with him. After this, he can do whatever with whoever he wants; I don't even care anymore.

I peek into the hallway only to find it empty. It's long and it looks like it continues around the corner. I know it's probably fruitless to look for him down here; there's no way he's still in this hallway, but I don't have any better ideas, so I try it anyway.

The hallway is almost eerie feeling; the only sound is the click of my heels on the tiled floor. I wander around for several minutes, exploring every passage I can to find Garret. Eventually, I find myself at a dead end.

There's a doorway in front of me. I turn the door handle and push, only to find myself outside, standing in three feet of snow. I am instantly mesmerized by the beauty of the forest. Each tree, from the pines to the oaks, is draped in a layer of snow. Their branches bend slightly, creating arches that look almost like doorways into the woods. The snow glistens on the ground as if it's covered in a layer of diamonds.

Suddenly, I hear a soft click behind me. "No," I whisper as I turn around. I was so distracted by the snowy wonderland in front of me that I allowed the door behind me to close. I try the handle in desperation, but it's locked. Great. I'm not wearing the right clothes to be in the snow. I didn't even bring my coat with me. I look down at my heels and shake my head. This is not going to be fun.

I wrap my arms around myself and begin to shiver. I have to get back inside quickly before hypothermia sets in. I begin the trek through the snow and around the building by taking large steps. With each step I take, my foot sinks down to the bottom, my heel getting lodged in the mud underneath the snow. To take my next step, I have to pull my heel out of the mud, fighting against the suction that is created between the mud and my heel. My progress is slow and with each passing minute, my fingers and toes get colder and colder.

No matter how hard I try to keep them on, I lose my shoes about halfway there.

I huff in frustration. I'm on the verge of tears as I stand there, trying to reach through the snow to find my shoes. It doesn't take long for me to realize it's not worth it. I have to keep going without them.

What feels like hours later, I finally get to an area of the resort that has been shoveled and breathe a sigh of relief. I made it. I walk quickly on the cleared ground to the front of the resort. My feet are now so cold they are numb.

I head through the front entrance of the resort into the main lobby. Almost immediately, a door behind the reception desk opens and out walks Miles. It's almost as if he was watching for me and knew I was coming in. I walk up to him.

"Hello, Mrs. Lawson," he says to me. "Is there anything I can do to help you?"

"Yes, maybe you can. I'm wondering if you've seen my husband. He disappeared when we were here earlier in the lobby and hasn't returned to our room."

"I have not seen him," he replies, his voice filled with genuine concern. "Is everything okay?"

I force a chuckle. "Yes, I'm sure everything's fine. He's probably already back in our room. I'm sorry for his rudeness earlier. He's just... going through some things."

"Please, don't even mention it. I had already forgotten," he says kindly.

"Thanks. You know, I am a little worried that he got lost or something," I say, trying to sound nonchalant.

"It is quite a big facility," he says. "It's easy to get lost in, especially if you go exploring in areas that are not meant for guests."

"Do you think you could send somebody to go find him? I mean, I don't want to look stupid if it's nothing, but I don't know, something just doesn't feel right."

"Yes, of course. I'll send our van driver to look for him. He's not leaving the property the rest of the day. There's supposed to be a storm blowing in."

"Thank you so much, Miles. I really appreciate it."

I look down at my bright red toes and my bright red

fingers, then back up at Miles with an embarrassed look on my face. "I lost my shoes in the snow," I say to explain my bare feet. "I was trying to find Garret, but got locked out of the building and had to walk around in the snowdrift." I shake my head. "It was stupid, really. I should have never let the door shut behind me."

"Oh no," Miles says. "I'll send someone looking for your shoes as well. I'm sure we can retrieve them."

"Please don't bother. They weren't that important to me. I have plenty more upstairs in my room."

"It's really not a problem," Miles says. "Our goal is for you to not have to lift a finger this weekend if we can help it. We'll bring them to you when we find them."

"Wow, okay. Thanks again for everything, Miles. I think I'll go back to my room now and wait there for Garret. I feel like the hot tub is calling my name."

"That sounds wonderful," Miles says. "Enjoy your stay."

I make my way back to our room. I open the door and walk inside the luxurious space. It has a spa-like feel and I decide that I'm not going to let Garret dictate whether or not I enjoy this weekend. Yes, I want our relationship to get better, but I'm not even sure that's possible anymore. He's been distant from me for so long. No matter what I try to do or how many conversations I have with him, it's always the same thing. He doesn't know what's wrong, just that he's not happy.

I can't fix something that I can't even name. Sometimes, I wonder if he hates me. He'll look at me with disgust in his eyes and I don't even know why. Yeah, I've let myself go a little bit, but I feel like I'm the same person for the most part that he married, yet he seems to loathe me most of the time.

I wish he would just remember what we once had together. I know that there's a kernel of love for me still in there somewhere. I just have to find it and nurture it, but I also know that if I'm the only one who cares about this relationship, then it's doomed to fail no matter how hard I try. Relationships take two people and I can't keep dragging both of us. If this weekend doesn't work, I'm going to have to let go and just take care of myself. Life is too short.

7

KORA (PAST)

I open the door to the tiny pub and it is packed. The small, dark space is standing room only. The sounds of a woman singing 80's music blasts on the loudspeakers. She's off-key and singing the wrong words, but the crowd doesn't care. They sing along with her at the top of their lungs.

I smile. I love karaoke. People who would normally never risk singing in front of other people take a chance and put themselves out there. Everyone cheers them on and nobody cares about perfection. I don't know. I think it just gives me hope that this world isn't beyond redemption to see strangers being supportive of each other instead of being judgmental.

There's also that rare time when someone will come to the stage and blow our socks off with their undiscovered talent. Some karaoke singers can sing better than most pop stars, especially here in Los Angeles. However, this woman is not an undiscovered pop star and I love it.

I immediately put in my request for a song before making my way to the bar. I spot my roommate Norma sitting there, animatedly talking to a man I've never seen before. I walk up behind her and wrap my arms around her. She jumps, then turns around.

"Kora," she screams. "You finally made it."

She wraps her arms around my neck and squeezes me hard. "Sorry for being late," I yell into her ear. "Who's your friend?"

She looks over at the guy she is talking to and stammers, trying to remember his name, but he saves her. "Ryan," he says.

"Kora, this is Ryan. Ryan, this is my best friend, Kora," Norma says with a smirk.

I shake his hand. "Nice to meet you."

"Likewise," he says.

Norma puts up her hand and places it on his chest. "Come find me later," she says. "Kora and I need to talk."

Ryan gets up off the stool, clearly knowing when he's no longer wanted. Norma pats the stool and insists that I sit next to her. As soon as I do, the bartender comes up and asks me for my order.

"Gin and tonic," I say. "With lime."

He nods and quickly begins making my drink. Norma puts her arm around my shoulders. "A gin and tonic occasion. I'm honored," she says.

"I'll need it," I joke.

"I feel like it's been forever since I've seen you," she says.

I laugh. "I saw you just this morning, Norma. What are you talking about?"

"I know, but we never talk anymore. I'm so glad you agreed to come out with me tonight."

"You know how much I love karaoke," I say. "I couldn't resist."

Suddenly, two drinks are placed in front of me. I look at the bartender quizzically. "I only ordered one," I say.

"The other one's from that guy at the end of the bar," he nods towards a brown-haired man sitting at the end of the bar with a hopeful look on his face. He smiles and waves at me, then gets up and walks towards me. Great. I can't go anywhere without having to fend these people off. "I just want a night out with my friend, not to be hit on by every guy in this bar," I yell to Norma.

She laughs. "It's crazy to me how many guys come up to you when we go out together. I may have one or two, but it's like ten for you. Minimum."

I shake my head. "I just don't even want to deal with it tonight," I tell her.

It doesn't take long before the guy is standing next to me. I grab the drink he bought for me and hand it to him. "Looks like they gave me your drink," I say, flashing him a smile.

"Oh no, that's for you," he says, flustered.

"I don't think so," I say. "I only ordered the one and I have a strict policy that I don't take drinks from strangers." I turn around, facing my back to him.

Norma stares at me, her eyes wide. "Wow, that was harsh," she whispers. She eyes the guy, who I'm guessing is still standing there, probably looking dejected and heart-broken. He'll get over it.

"I know it sounds bad, but I don't know if I care," I tell her. "I can't be worrying about these guys' feelings, especially when I gave him no indication that I even wanted to talk to him. I'm just not in the mood tonight, I guess."

I glance over my shoulder and see the guy walking away, his shoulders hunched. I feel a pang of guilt. I probably should have been nicer to him.

Norma and I manage to have an uninterrupted conversation for maybe thirty minutes before I'm approached by a different man. This time, however, he just boldly walks right up to me and taps me on the shoulder.

"Excuse me," he says.

I turn around, annoyed at first, but as soon as I see him, my breath catches in my throat. He's probably one of the most handsome men I've ever seen. His eyes are blue and flecked with gold in the center. It's obvious that he's probably a decade older than me. His blondish hair is slightly gray at the temples and there are tiny little wrinkles around his eyes, which I think adds to his charm. This is the type of man I would want to get to know better, but I can't make it too easy on him.

"You're stunning. I couldn't help but notice you across the room and well, I just wanted to know if I could have your number and call you sometime."

"That's how you do it, huh?" I ask him. "Just walk up to a girl and ask her for her number. Do I look crazy?" I ask.

He looks flustered. "No, I'm sorry. I guess I'm just kind of out of practice."

"Well, people don't just give out their number to people they don't know," I tell him. "We might connect on social media, but even then, I have to feel like I know you a little bit. I don't even know your name."

The man opens his mouth to reply when my name is called over the loudspeaker. "You'll have to excuse me," I say, stopping him before he can speak. "I'll be right back."

I walk up to the stage, nerves causing my fingers to tingle and a fluttering feeling to erupt in my stomach. It's been a while since I've done this, but as the music starts, muscle memory takes over and I start to sing.

When I was a kid, all I wanted was to be a singer. I came

to L.A. when I was nineteen with two thousand dollars in my backpack and barely a week's worth of clothes.

After my first year of college, I just knew that the academic path was not for me. I worked all summer to save up as much money as I could so I could follow my real dreams. I was young and naive. Two thousand dollars didn't last me long. I got a job as a waitress, but I wanted nothing more than to sing professionally. My job, while usually accommodating, made me miss opportunities and my dream felt further and further away over time.

That was almost a decade ago. I now work in an office as a secretary and my dreams of being a singer have been almost completely dashed by the harshness of this city. It seems like you have to nearly sell yourself to the devil to make it here. I guess I wasn't willing to do that.

When my song is over, I walk back towards Norma and the guy. He's looking at me with complete shock and adoration. "You were amazing," he says.

"Oh, it was nothing," I tell him. "You should see me when I actually try," I smirk and sit back on the stool.

"Great job, as always," says Norma. She leans over to the guy. "Don't let her be too modest. She's the best singer in the room. I always tell her that she should be on Broadway or something like that."

"You don't have to tell me. I was blown away," he says.

Red heat rushes to my face and I fold my hands on my lap. As much as I like the attention I get when I'm on stage, this kind of attention makes me cringe in embarrassment. Maybe that's why I usually don't even give guys a chance. Apart from singing, I hate being the center of attention.

"Hey," Norma says, interrupting my musings. "You know that guy I was talking to earlier?"

I nod.

She continues. "I think we're going to go grab a few drinks somewhere else. Are you going to be okay here by yourself?"

I glance over at the strange man sitting next to me, then nod and give her a big hug. "I'll see you at home."

"Thanks, Kora. Love you," she says. She pulls away, grabs her purse and gets up.

The guy immediately sits in her now empty seat. "So, tell me about yourself," he says.

"Why should I tell you anything about myself when I don't even know your name?"

He reaches out his hand to shake mine. "Garret."

"Kora," I say, grabbing his hand. "So, what brings you to L.A.?"

Garret smiles, his eyes lighting up with a touch of genuine excitement. "Business," he replies. "I'm here for some meetings and to explore potential opportunities to expand."

"That sounds exciting. What field are you in?" I lean towards him.

"I own my own sales company," he says with a hint of pride. "It's fairly new, but I sell medical equipment to doctors and hospitals."

I nod, impressed. "That sounds both challenging and rewarding," I comment.

Garret chuckles. "It definitely has its ups and downs, but I find it fulfilling. What about you, Kora? Is music your passion?"

Embarrassment rushes through me yet again. "It used to be," I reply, a sad smile gracing my lips. "Music has always been my sanctuary, my way of expressing myself, but I guess you could say that this city has beaten me down. I don't sing much anymore."

He leans in closer, his eyes locked with mine. "You shouldn't give up so easily," he says sincerely. "Your voice is captivating, Kora."

A blush creeps up my cheeks, his words touching a chord deep within me. "Thank you, Garret. That means a lot to me."

We continue talking to each other for what feels like hours, the conversation flowing effortlessly between us. At first, we have to yell over the karaoke, but once the singing stops and the regular bar music resumes, it's easier to hear each other. We have so much in common. It's crazy. Our love for classical music, movies and eighties pop music dominates much of our conversation.

I feel myself relaxing around him and by the end of the night, I realize that I don't want the evening to end. I grab a napkin from a stack on the bar and a pen from my purse. I write down my phone number and pass it to him.

He looks at me, surprised. "I didn't think you gave out your number."

"I guess I'm willing to make an exception," I say. "There's something about you that makes me feel safe. I don't know. Maybe it's stupid."

He grabs my hand and stares into my eyes. "It's not stupid. You're safe with me."

8

AMELIA (PRESENT)

I pace anxiously around the room. It's been at least two hours and there's still no sign of Garret. He should have been back by now. Does he think I'm stupid? Maybe I'm reading too much into it. Obviously, he got lost on his way back.

I've called the front desk several times and each time, Miles reassures me that they have people looking for him. I don't know what that means exactly. Are the staff just keeping an eye out for him as they go about their daily business, or are they actively looking? It's probably the first thing. Nobody has time to hunt down a grown man.

My musings are interrupted by the ringing of the telephone in the room. I quickly walk over to it, answering it after only the second ring. "Hello," I say.

"Mrs. Lawson? It's Miles from the front desk."

"Yes, hi, Miles," I say nervously.

"I believe one of our staff has found your husband. They're bringing him to the lobby if you want to meet us down here."

Relief floods through me. "Is he okay?"

"I'm not exactly sure of the details, but I promise we'll look into it."

"Thank you so much, Miles," I say, hanging up the phone. I look at the clock. We have an hour until dinner. It's hard not to be mad at Garret for doing something so foolish and chasing after that woman. What if he found her and they were doing something... my mind doesn't even want to go there.

I rush down to the lobby only to find it empty, except for Miles standing behind the desk. I quickly walk over to him. "Where's Garret?" I ask breathlessly.

"I'm sorry, Mrs. Lawson. He'll be here in a few minutes. Apparently, he got himself locked in an area of the resort that was not renovated. One of the staff members had to go to the back office and hunt for the key. It's not something we keep on hand."

"What?" I say, confused. "He was locked in a room somewhere?"

"Technically, a prison block," Miles says. "It's similar to the one that you're staying in, but nothing has been upgraded in it yet. It's the next thing on our plans if this opening weekend goes well."

I shake my head. Only a stupid person would accidentally get locked in a prison cell.

Moments later, Garret enters the lobby, looking haggard and angry. "Did you hear what happened to me?" He asks the moment he lays eyes on me.

"Yes, Garret, how did you get yourself locked in a cell like that?"

"Somebody locked me in. It wasn't an accident. The door was propped open; there was no way it could have closed on its own. I was looking in one of the cells and the next thing I knew, I heard the door shut. I tried getting out, but I couldn't."

"You think somebody did this to you on purpose?" I say incredulously.

"Yes, there's no other way it could have happened. Besides, what kind of resort has places that their guests can go that can get them locked away?"

Miles interjects, attempting to diffuse this situation. "Mr. Lawson, I completely understand your concerns. However, there are several signs clearly indicating that the area is off-limits to guests. We take safety very seriously here and we do our best to prevent incidents like this. With that said, we do expect that you pay attention to the signs we post."

I place a hand on Garret's arm. "Just let it go, Garret. Nothing bad happened to you, other than a few lost hours. It's not worth it."

Garret crosses his arms, contemplating my words.

I continue. "We have dinner in less than forty-five minutes. Let's not dwell on this now. We can address it with management later if necessary."

Garret relents, his frustration etched on his face. "Fine," he grumbles, "let's get back to the room and get ready for dinner."

As we make our way to the room, the tension between us hangs in the air. I silently hope that when he sees how beautiful the room is and all of the amenities, he will quickly forget the last few hours. However, as soon as we enter the grand foyer, Garret's face turns to anger once more.

"They have us staying in one of these? This is the same kind of place I got locked in," he exclaims.

"It's really nice, Garret, I promise. It's one of the most exquisite rooms I've ever stayed in."

"We're staying in a prison cell," he says, his frustration evident. "I don't care what you do to it. It's still a prison cell."

I shake my head sadly. This isn't gonna go well.

We trudge up the two flights of stairs to our room. I unlock the door and slide it open, hopeful that as soon as he steps inside, he will change his mind. Garret steps into the room and I stand behind him, eagerly awaiting his reaction. He stands in the middle of the room and scans it, his expression unchanging.

"You're not impressed?" I ask, deflated. "I thought you'd love it."

Garret lets out a sigh as he scans the room again. "Yeah, it's nice," he replies dismissively. "But I've seen better and I can't get over the fact that we're sleeping in a prison cell."

I shake my head sadly. Can't he just be happy for once? Can't he find this as an adventure and not a completely torturous experience? I feel like he doesn't actually want to make our marriage better. He's only here to placate me and make it look like he tried, but he has no intentions of putting in any real effort.

Garret looks at the bags on the floor and then back at me. "Where's our fifth bag?"

"Remember, they couldn't find it? They're still looking."

"Great," he says. "All my good shirts are in that missing bag. I don't know what I'm going to do to get ready for dinner if it doesn't come."

"You have nothing in your other bag?" I ask, disappointed.

"Maybe a couple of shirts, but not much," he grumbles. He walks straight towards the bar and pours himself a drink.

I sigh. If today is any indication, this weekend is going to be a disaster.

I grab one of my suitcases, set it on the bed and unzip it.

I pull out a navy blue floor-length gown. This will do. I bought it because it accentuates my waist and hips — things about me that Garret used to love. I had hoped that I could reignite his desire for me in this dress, but now, I'm not sure it will do any good.

I quickly slip into the dress and pull my hair into a nice bun. It's simple yet elegant. I adjust my makeup and add a strand of pearls around my neck. I double-check my appearance in the bathroom mirror. I look good. I'm reminded of the woman that I was when I got married. I should have never let myself go as much as I have.

Standing here in my dress and makeup, I feel elegant and confident in a way that I haven't felt in a long time. I want to hold on to this feeling. Even if Garret and I don't make it out of this weekend, maybe, just maybe, I can rediscover myself.

9

KORA (PAST)

I rifle through my makeup bag, looking for my mascara. I can hear Garret banging pots and pans around in the kitchen. He insisted that this morning he was going to make me breakfast and the noise in the kitchen is evidence that he's at least trying. I smirk at the thought. I've never seen him cook the entire time we've been dating.

The last couple of months have been some of the happiest of my life. Since that moment we met at the bar, Garret and I have become almost inseparable. He flies in here every week on Monday morning and then leaves on Friday afternoon to go back home to Las Vegas. He works during the day, but in the evenings, we spend every second that we can together.

I expertly apply the mascara to my eyelashes, then take a step back from the mirror, pleased with what I see. I'm going on an audition today. Garret has been encouraging me to get back into my music. I was reluctant at first because I had been rejected so many times before, but he's helped me find the courage again to put myself out there.

I'm not auditioning for anything amazing, just an in-house singing position at a local restaurant. They play live music on Fridays, Saturdays and Sundays and their band needs a lead singer. It's not exactly worldwide famous, but it's a start. Who knows, if I get this gig, I could be discovered by somebody eating at the restaurant. All it takes is one person to give me a chance.

The thought of getting back out there fills me with a mixture of excitement and hope, tinged with a bit of anxiety. I don't know if I can take much more rejection. It's been a long time since I've even been willing to be vulnerable like this. My skin isn't very thick. "You got this. You were born for this. Just go out there and be yourself," I whisper to my reflection in an attempt to pump myself up.

I smooth down my cream-colored dress and take one last look in the mirror before exiting the bathroom. As soon as I open the door, the smell of pancakes wafts in from the kitchen. Garret is singing at the top of his lungs and trust me, he should never audition for a singing role. He is off-key and loud and I love it.

A smile forms on my lips as I round the corner into the kitchen. He's standing at the stove, wearing only his boxer shorts, nothing else. The muscles on his bare chest are flexing as he moves with a sense of purpose, flipping pancakes and expertly placing them on a plate.

I lean against the doorframe, cross my arms and smile. My heart flutters at the sight of him. How did I get so lucky? I only wish he could be here all the time. I wish he didn't have to go back every weekend.

Sometimes, I wonder what he's going back to and why he can't just stay. I know he has a place back there that he needs to take care of, but I can't help the small little doubt that tickles the back of my mind. I push it aside. "Looking good, babe," I say to him. He startles and looks at me as if he's just now noticing that I'm standing there.

"Whoa," he says. "You look amazing."

"Thanks. I have that audition today, remember?" I reply.

"Right," he says. "I wish I could be here for you when you get back. I have to leave this morning, you know."

The thought of him leaving makes me sad, but I force myself to dismiss it. I'm determined to make the most out of breakfast this morning. I walk up to him and wrap my arms around his back. "You don't have to go, you know. You could just stay here for the weekend." I force myself to keep my tone playful and light. The last thing I want is for him to feel pressured.

He turns around and wraps his arm around my neck, still holding the spatula in one hand. "Kora, you know I can't do that. I have obligations back home that I have to take care of. I have to water my plants, feed my goldfish and check in on my mom, plus other things that I have to do."

I try not to look sad, but I can't help it. I want more from him. Maybe it's time that I broach the topic and at least ask. I take a deep breath and find the courage to speak. "I've been thinking."

"About what, babe?" He asks kindly.

"We've been hanging out like this for a couple of months and I have loved every second of it. It seems to me that we're getting a little bit more serious. I mean, this is the first time that you've ever made me breakfast."

He grabs my face and kisses me lightly, then pulls away. "You know how much I care about you, Kora. And I want nothing more than to spend even the weekends with you, but I just can't yet."

"I know," I say. "I'm not trying to push you into something you're not ready to do, Garret. I'm just wondering when I can get breakfast like this on a regular basis," I say, forcing a smile to my lips.

Garret grins playfully, a spark of mischievousness dancing in his eyes. "What makes you think breakfast is the only trick I have up my sleeve?" He asks.

I stare up at him, overwhelmed by a surge of affection and what I think might be love for this man. I'm not ready or willing to say it out loud, but I want nothing more than for him to be mine permanently.

We stare into each other's eyes for what feels like hours before he leans down and kisses me deeply. I kiss him back with everything I have inside of me.

Suddenly, a burning smell interrupts our moment. I push away from him. "Garret, the pancakes."

"Crap," he says, turning around quickly and lifting them off the pan with a spatula. He then looks at me sheepishly. "Do you want to go out to breakfast?"

I smile and laugh. "Sounds like a plan."

10

AMELIA (PRESENT)

I peek my head out of the bathroom, only to find Garret still sitting on the bed, looking dejected. "What are you doing?" I ask, frustrated.

He slowly looks over at me and then back at his drink. "I don't have anything to wear," he says pathetically. "I'm not going."

I shake my head. "Of course you're going." I stomp over to his suitcase and throw it on the bed, opening it up. Within seconds, I find three shirts, two pairs of slacks and a tie. I lay them on the bed neatly next to him. "Look, you have choices," I say. "Not everything was in that other suitcase."

He glances at the clothes and then up at me, a look of resignation in his eyes.

"What is up with you, Garret? I get that you don't like this place and you don't really want to be here, but why are you being so obstinate? What happened earlier today? Why did you take off like that?"

"I told you I had to go to the bathroom."

"There's a bathroom in our room. There was no reason to go down that hallway to hunt for one."

He shrugs. "I guess it was an emergency."

Lies. I can see them all over his face, but no matter how much I push, I know he's not going to tell me. This is how our marriage has been for a while now.

There was a long period of time when he was leaving every week for work. He would come home on weekends, but during the week, I could barely reach him. I hated it. It was as if he was living a completely separate life apart from me. I could feel him pulling away from me and our marriage slipping through the cracks.

That all stopped a few months ago. His business trips are less frequent now and shorter, but our marriage hasn't gotten any better. It's almost as if he can't stand the sight of me now. And I don't know what to do to fix it.

Suddenly, there's a loud clanging sound on our prison door. Garret gets up slowly from the bed and walks towards it, opening it just a crack to see who is outside.

"Mr. Lawson," a deep voice says.

"Yes?" Garret replies.

"I have your bag for you."

Garret looks down at the man's hands and then he pulls the door fully open. "Took you guys long enough," Garret says rudely.

A look of irritation flits across the man's face and then slowly disappears.

"Thank you so much, sir," I say.

"You may call me Bruce," he interjects.

"Thank you, Bruce. Where did you find it?" I ask curiously.

"It somehow got lost in a drift of snow near a walkway.

I'm not sure how, but it took me hours to find it," Bruce explains.

"Oh, wow," I say. "You didn't have to go to all that trouble."

"Yes, he did. They lost it. They had a responsibility to find it," Garret says, clearly still way too annoyed about the situation.

"Don't worry, Mr. Lawson, I wasn't going to stop until I found it. We pride ourselves on the highest quality service here."

"It should have never gotten lost in the first place," Garret retorts. "Your man should have been more careful."

Bruce glares at Garret. "Sometimes bags get lost, just like people. Who knows why it happens? But all I know is it happens when you least expect it."

Bruce's words are ominous, as if he might have been the one who locked Garret in that cell. No, it couldn't have been on purpose like Garret thinks it was. No one would do that, especially to a guest.

"What are you trying to say?" Garret asks.

"Nothing," Bruce says. "I hope you enjoy your stay, Mr. and Mrs. Lawson."

He backs out of the room and closes the door behind him.

"Did you hear that?" Garret says, turning to me. "I think he was the one who locked me in the cell."

"Why would he do that, Garret? He doesn't even know you."

"I don't know, but it seemed pretty obvious to me by his words and tone of voice. *People go missing?*" he says, mocking Bruce's voice. "He tried to make me go missing. I just know it."

"You're ridiculous and reading something into nothing.

That man might be gruff, but he didn't lock you in a cell. You just want to be mad about this situation so that you don't have to try to have a good time with me this weekend."

"That's not true," Garret says. "Somebody really did lock me in that cell, I swear! And I have every right to be mad about it."

"Whatever," I say, heading back into the bathroom. I don't have time to keep arguing with him. "Be ready to go in ten minutes," I yell from the bathroom. "I don't want to be late."

11

KORA (PAST)

So much has changed since my first audition back. I booked that gig and I've been working every weekend since then. Within a few weeks, I was getting offers to do gigs all around town. There were so many requests that I had to hire an agent to help me field them all. I'm almost to the point where I can quit my day job, maybe just a couple more months.

I stare at my calendar for the upcoming week and shake my head. I'm booked nearly every night this week. Some of them are private party engagements, while others are gigs at local bars and restaurants.

The band from my weekend gig has started coming with me everywhere I go. They're great, honestly. I couldn't have done this without them. We often have jam sessions on the weekends, where we write new songs and practice the ones we already know. We started off just being a cover band of popular eighties and nineties hits, but in the last few weeks, we've tested out some of our original songs and the crowds seem to love them.

This is the life I have always dreamed of having here in L.A. and after those first few years, I never expected to get it.

I wouldn't have been able to do it without Garret. He still comes to see me every week, but now we spend our nights out at the bars or restaurants where I'm playing my gigs. He's the best groupie ever. Just last Thursday night, I performed at a famous local bar. The crowd went wild for us. When it was over, I left the stage on such a high.

Garret came to find me backstage immediately after it ended. He threw his arms around me and gave me a huge kiss. "I'm so proud of you, Kora. I can't believe how far you've come in just the last few months. You were destined for this."

I smiled at him and basked in the warmth of his praise. This man gets me. He can see my heart and he encourages it. Why couldn't I have found him ten years ago when I was starting out on this journey? I could be so far by now, just with his encouragement. I try not to think back on those years with regret.

I've learned and grown so much from the struggles that I faced. Maybe that's what it was all about. Maybe I couldn't handle the pressure of this mounting fame when I was younger. I needed to grow up first. I had to learn responsibility and patience before being given this opportunity. There's no use dwelling on the past and wishing it was different. Different may not have been better. I could have ruined my entire chance if I had been given this opportunity ten years ago.

I pull up my laptop and type in the password. I immediately go to my email inbox and see five messages from my agent. Each one is an individual gig that I've been requested to play at. One of them catches my eye. She thinks it would be a good idea for me to go on tour, something small at first, singing backup. It would be around the northern United States. Based on her plan, it would be three or four months long and cover fifty cities. Wow. This is more than I could ever have imagined or hoped for just a year ago.

Norma walks into the room and sees the expression on my face. "What's going on?" She asks.

I look up at her. "I'm gonna go on tour."

"What?" She asks.

"It's nothing big, but it's a tour."

"That's amazing, Kora. I'm so happy for you."

Tears form in my eyes as the reality of what my future could possibly look like sinks in. "I think I've done it, Norma. I think I've finally done it."

She sits next to me and wraps her arms around me. "I never doubted for one second that you were going to eventually make it. You just had to work up the courage to get out there again. I knew that once people really heard your voice, there was no way they were going to be able to say no."

"They said no lots of times," I laugh through the tears. "Don't you remember how many times I came home rejected?"

"Yeah, but they've never heard this Kora. This Kora has become something special."

"I couldn't have done it without your crazy self forcing me to all those karaoke nights. I swear they made me more relaxed and ultimately better."

"See? I knew there was a reason you had to go to those," she says.

I shake my head. "I love you, Norma."

"Love you back, girl," she says, exiting my room.

I turn my attention back to my laptop and take a moment to check my social media accounts. They have also grown exponentially in the last few months. I have thousands of new followers; it's overwhelming. For the most part, I allow anyone to follow me on social media, except for on my Chatbook account. I've decided to keep that private as a way of interacting with my family and friends without having to provide all the details to the public.

I check my Chatbook account. There are several posts from my mom. She does the funniest thing when she uses social media. She'll post something that she likes to her wall. If she really likes it, several minutes later, she'll come back and press the like button on her own post. And then she'll share it again on her wall just a few hours later, just to make sure that we saw it. I guess it's one way to make sure your message gets across. It always makes me chuckle.

After a few minutes of scrolling through the multitude of duplicate posts my mom has made, I notice a friend request in the corner of the app. I click on the request and find that it's from a woman whose name I recognize, but I've never met: Cathy Whitman.

The last time I talked to my mom, she wouldn't shut up about Cathy. Her profile picture is of a cat, a tabby cat, if I'm not mistaken. My mom even showed me her profile and all the funny cat pictures Cathy had posted. At first, I was a little suspicious that Cathy was a real person. She hadn't made very many posts and all of them happened in the last few months. The most suspicious thing to me, though, was her profile picture. I almost never trust someone whose picture is not of their face. I always wonder what they're hiding.

I mentioned my concerns to my mom and she dismissed them immediately. She made it sound like she and Cathy were best friends. I'm not quite sure where they met, but it was probably at the weekly bingo event my mom attends religiously at the city hall of her small town. She is so outgoing, always making new friends at bingo.

Every time she goes there, she talks about me nonstop. When I go back home to visit her, I'm often bombarded by old ladies wanting to know every detail about my life. I've gotten used to being the subject of their daily gossip sessions. I go ahead and approve the request from Cathy.

I close the laptop and take a deep breath, forcing myself to focus on the prospect of going on tour. After a few minutes, reality sinks in. If I'm going to be singing on stage, night after night, I can't be out of breath. I need to work out and build up some stamina. I put on my yoga pants and a large T-shirt and head out the door for the gym.

"I'll be back in about an hour," I yell to Norma.

"Okay," she yells back from her room.

12

AMELIA (PRESENT)

I'm putting on the finishing touches of my makeup as I run through the events of the day. How did the day go so sideways? I thought that if we just got away from the busyness of life and made some effort to put time into each other, we could remember who we once were together. However, Garret has fought me at every turn. It's as if he wants us to break up. It seems as if no part of him wants us to reconcile and come back together.

Grief threatens to grip my heart and overwhelm me. I try to stop them, but the tears begin to well up inside, threatening to spill over and ruin my makeup. I don't know what to do anymore. It takes two people to make a marriage work. I can't be the only one fighting for this.

I think about the gift I have tucked away in one of my suitcases for Garret. I wanted to get him something that would remind him of who he once was and the passions he used to have that he's let fall away. I consider giving it to him now. Maybe it will do what I have been unable to do since we left. It feels like a Hail Mary, but I have no other options.

From the bathroom door, I see Garret steaming his white

dress shirt. His muscular chest is bare and it's obvious he has worked hard to continue taking care of himself. The sight of him takes my breath away; even all these years later, I'm still attracted to my husband.

I just wish my heart was as easy to diagnose. The truth is, I'm not sure if I'm trying so desperately to make this work because I actually still love him or if I'm just trying not to fail. I want to love him. I want to feel those sparks that once flew between us, but these days, I just feel dead inside. It's almost as if his absence and neglect have stripped me of every ounce of emotion I once had toward him. Now, I just feel a sense of duty and obligation to stay the course. I can't give up.

A frantic thought enters my mind and without thinking, I quickly start digging through his bag. Why would he care so much if the bag was missing for just a few moments? I rustle around clothes and scan a few items, before I snap myself out of it. What if he catches me going through his stuff? This is just not worth it. I am reaching for anything just to feel something again.

I keep hoping and praying that I'll find those secure, romantic feelings deep inside me this weekend. I want us to rediscover what was once there together. Actually, no, I don't even need us to go back to what we once were. I don't even know if I have the energy for that young, puppy-type love again, but I believe we could find a more mature love for each other, the kind my grandparents had.

They were married for fifty years. Of course, their life was hard and things between them were not always great, but they survived. They were so tender towards each other in the end, always holding each other's hands and caring for each other. Their love wasn't passionate, but it was kind, sweet and gentle. As I get older, that's what I want: someone I know who has my back in sickness, not just health. Someone who cherishes me deeply. Someone to call for help if I fall down the stairs in our house. Is that too much to ask?

I grab my bag and find the present I had wrapped for Garret for our anniversary. I'm nervous and excited to give it to him. I hope that he sees the potential it can bring him to come back to himself and reignite a passion that he once had.

"I have something for you, Garret," I say.

He sets down the steamer and turns towards me. "What is it?" He asks gruffly.

I walk over to him and hand him the present. "I got this for you for our anniversary. I hope you like it."

He grabs it from me, confused. "I thought this trip was our present to each other."

"I know, but I saw this and I thought of you. I just really wanted you to have it."

"Okay," he says hesitantly, sitting on the bed. He opens it. Underneath the wrapping paper is an unmarked box. He takes his keys out of his pocket and uses them to cut the tape. As soon as he opens it, I fully expect his expression to change into one of joy. It doesn't. He just stares at what's in the box.

"What is this?" He asks.

I grab it from him and take out the object. "It's a vintage camera," I tell him. "Don't you remember how passionate you were about taking pictures? I found the exact same camera you had when we first met. I was also able to find at least fifty rolls of film for it too."

"Do they even still develop that kind of film?"

"There's a place about thirty minutes from our house that will still do it. I made sure."

"I haven't thought about photography since we got married. Once I realized that anybody could take pictures with the cameras on their phones and they turned out almost as good as the ones I took with that thing, it kind of lost its appeal for me. Have you never wondered why I quit?"

"No," I say dejectedly. "I guess I just assumed it was because we got busy and then there was your company. And then the camera went missing in one of our moves. I don't know, maybe it was stupid of me to get it for you. I just thought that maybe it would help you reignite your passion for something I thought made you so happy."

He shakes his head. "No, I didn't quit just because I got too busy. I quit because I figured, what's the point? When everybody can do the thing you're doing, it makes you not special. Why spend hours practicing something a kid could do with their phone?"

"There's definitely a difference between a picture taken on a phone and a professional photographer. It's ridiculous to think that they're the same," I push back.

"There may be some minor quality differences, but those are not enough for the average person to be able to even notice them. And now, with the editing software, even those differences are shrinking. I just can't compete, so I stopped trying," he says, putting the camera back in the box and setting it beside the bed, not even bothering to really look at it.

His indifference is like a knife to my chest. Why do I even try with this man? Everything I do is counted as meaningless to him. He hasn't even noticed my dress, my hair, or my makeup. It's as if I don't even exist in his world.

He stands and walks to his suitcase, rifling around in it.

"I mean, since we're on the topic of dreams, are you going to apply to NextGen this year?"

I sit on the bed, dejected as his words settle in. After meeting a VP at a tech conference last year, I made such an impression that she gave me an open offer from the tech conglomerate. I just never pulled the trigger. Garret wouldn't understand why. No one could.

He reads my face and chooses to drop it. A few seconds later, he walks over and stands in front of me. "I'm not a complete jerk," he says.

I look up at him, confused.

He shoves a black box in my face. "I did get you something for our anniversary. I was just thinking I was going to be the only one and I would look like a hero," he chuckles.

I take the box from him and stare at it in shock. Did he really think of me ahead of time? I slowly open the lid to reveal a dainty silver necklace with a large jade pendant hanging in the center.

"Oh my gosh. It's beautiful. You got this for me?" I say, looking up at him.

"Yes. Do you like it?" He asks gruffly.

"I love it," I stand and hand it to him. "Would you put it on me?"

He nods.

I turn around and he reaches around me, laying the pendant on my chest and then clasping the necklace behind my neck. I grab it with one hand and turn around. "Thank you, Garret. This means so much to me."

He wraps his arms around me in the first embrace I remember him giving me all weekend. I return the hug and I can feel a kernel of hope blossom inside of me. Maybe this weekend isn't lost after all and maybe, just maybe, we could save our marriage.

I pull away from him. "We gotta go, Garret. We're late for dinner. Did you, by any chance, check in with the sitter?" I ask him, realizing that we haven't even let them know we arrived safely.

"No, I didn't. I'm sorry."

"That's okay." I grab my phone and send a quick text message, letting them know that we are safe and asking how the cat is doing.

I don't wait for a response, but instead, I grab my purse, slip my phone into it and then glance at the camera sitting by the bed. I decide to grab it also. Maybe I'll take up photography myself since Garret is no longer interested. Maybe giving myself a hobby will help me find more meaning and purpose in life. Not that my life isn't meaningful, but sometimes I feel like I have lost myself by only being invested in starting a family and nothing else for years. I need something more. Even if Garret and I don't reconnect, maybe it's something I can do for myself.

I place my purse strap over my shoulder and turn to look at Garret. His shirt is on now and he looks as handsome as the day we got married. "You ready?" I ask.

He grabs my hand and opens the door. We exit our hotel room into the open air of the cell block and for the first time tonight, I'm excited about what lies ahead.

13

AMELIA

I walk into the dining room and it takes my breath away. They have somehow transformed the prison mess hall into an upscale and exclusive-looking dining area. Chandeliers hang from the ceiling and thick burgundy drapes cover the windows. In the far corner of the room, a string quartet plays, creating an ambiance of elegance that is unexpected considering the location. They've covered the floors with rich, dark mahogany wood, which adds to the high-class ambiance.

The maître d' escorts us to our table towards the front of the room. The table is covered in a crisp white linen. On top of the tablecloth, several candles are lit inside glass jars decorated with a swirling black and white design on the outside. They are artfully arranged around a basket of bread.

Garret pulls out my chair for me and I look at him in shock. Where has this man been for years? "Thank you," I say, allowing him to push it back in.

He walks to his side of the table and sits across from me.

"This is nice, right?" I say to him.

He nods. "I gotta say, I never imagined they could pull a room like this off in a prison."

"Right? It's honestly astonishing."

I look around the room and am surprised at how empty it looks. "Kind of weird that there's not very many people here," I tell Garret.

He scans the room himself and nods. "Yeah, it's kinda strange. Especially, since we're all supposed to eat dinner at the same time."

On the far side of the room, I see the head concierge, Miles, making his way to each table to greet the guests. I grab a piece of bread and expertly apply a thin layer of butter. I take a bite while Garret does the same. "Wow, this sourdough is delicious. I wonder how old their starter is for it to have such a rich flavor," I muse.

Garret looks at me as if I've lost my mind. "What are you even talking about, Amelia?"

"Never mind, it's not important." I could try to explain it to him, but I know he would only be half-listening and I would just end up frustrated with his lack of attention.

After a few minutes, Miles finally makes it to our table. "Mr. and Mrs. Lawson," he says. "I hope things have settled down since the incident this afternoon."

I nod. "Yes, we're doing fine. Thank you for all your help."

"And you've got your bag back?" He asks Garret.

"Yes, thank you," says Garret, reluctantly.

"Miles, I'm curious," I say to him. "How come this space is so empty? Especially since dinner is served to everyone at the same time, I just thought it would be more full than this."

"Oh, it will be eventually, but the soft opening this

weekend was a pretty exclusive event. You had to have a direct invite to come," Miles explains.

Garret looks at me, surprised. "Who invited you?"

"I found the invitation on social media. I just assumed that it was a public invitation," I reply.

Miles shakes his head. "No, we allowed people to advertise to their friends and family, but that was it. So you should feel lucky to be here."

"Wow," I say. "I had no idea. I do feel lucky."

"Well, anyway, that's the reason why most of these tables are empty," Miles says. "We wanted to give our guests a world-class experience, so we limited the numbers to make sure that every guest felt special."

Suddenly, waiters begin entering from the side doors, each carrying a large tray of food.

"We don't even get to order what we want at this event?" Garret asks incredulously.

Miles shakes his head. "No, I'm sorry, but be assured, it is a finely crafted menu by our world-renowned chef. I'm sure you'll enjoy it."

I look over at Garret. "Can you just be in the moment and have fun? Why do you have to criticize everything?"

Miles takes that as his cue to exit and walk to another table.

"I don't think this is an exclusive event," Garret says. "They just weren't ready to handle that many tourists at one time. So they're making you feel like you're special when you're not."

"You don't know that," I say. "Why can't you just be quiet and enjoy yourself for once?"

The waiter places our plates in front of us. Both of us have a perfectly cooked ribeye steak, charred around the edges, just as Garret likes it. On the side is grilled asparagus shining with butter and lemon, as well as a generous portion of creamy mashed potatoes.

Garret picks up his fork and knife, slices a bite of the steak and puts it in his mouth. "Wow, that's amazing," he says.

"See," I say. "This is world-class. They did give me a dinner option survey; it's not like they'd force you to eat red meat if you don't. You need to learn to just let go and have fun."

"Fine," he says. "I'll stop being so critical. I honestly can't remember the last time that I've had a steak this perfect."

"Is it better than that place we went to in Seattle?" I ask.

"La Trattoria? Let's not talk crazy now," he smirks.

I smile. What's crazy is how quickly he can change back to the charming Garret I fell in love with.

He continues. "But I would say this food is at about the level of what they served us on the hyperloop, when we took the train up to Seattle."

Now he's reminiscing with me. This trip might have been all that we needed.

Our conversation at dinner starts off good and devolves into mundane. We talk about Garret's business and I update him on the new, quirky products at the grocery store. The subject of our relationship is never broached, even though it lingers in the back of my mind. I just don't know what the point is anymore. I could try to beg him to be more present like I've done so many times in the past, but it's always just fallen on deaf ears.

We finish our plates and a busboy comes by to grab them for us. Several minutes later, out comes our dessert — rich, dark chocolate mousse with raspberries and whipped cream. We take the first few bites of our dessert when Miles walks on stage to make an announcement. "I hope you all have been enjoying your evening and this amazing food prepared by Chef Bond," he says.

The crowd claps their hands in recognition of the meal they just ate.

Miles continues. "Well, now you are all in for a treat. Tonight's entertainment will be performed by Kora Mendez, an up-and-coming artist whose popularity is skyrocketing worldwide."

I look over at Garret. His face is stark white. "Are you okay? Are you sick?" I ask.

He shakes his head. "I'm fine," he says, but I can tell he's not. He purses his lips and stares at Kora as she walks up to the stage. I look in her direction. She's tall and beautiful. She's dressed elegantly in a white, floor-length gown. She looks almost as if she was transported from a different era.

Garret's white face has now turned beet red and I can't tell if it's an expression of anger or sadness. No matter what it is, he is trying desperately to hide it.

"You don't look so well," I tell him as Kora begins singing in the background.

"I don't feel well," he stammers.

14

AMELIA

Garret's eyes remain transfixed on Kora throughout her song, while my eyes dart back and forth between them. It's obvious something is going on, simmering beneath the surface. It dawns on me — she's the woman that Garret followed down the hallway. How could he be so blatantly obvious? It's true; he hasn't been very attentive to me in years, but he's never so blatantly ignored the fact that I exist and am sitting right next to him. It's almost as if he doesn't even care anymore if I know what he's doing.

I stare at the woman on stage for several seconds before it hits. Clasped around her neck is a jade necklace identical to mine. My hand flies to my necklace and I wrap my fist around the pendant.

A red-hot embarrassment flushes my face and I glance at Garret. There's no way this is a coincidence. Why does this woman have the exact same necklace as me? Could he really have been foolish enough to get his wife and his mistress the same necklace?

Fear knots my stomach as I think about the possibilities.

How long has this affair been going on? The entire time she's singing, Kora never even looks in our direction. It's as if she's avoiding our table entirely. Garret's eyes never leave her as a whole host of emotions display on his face, betraying his thoughts.

As soon as the song is over, Kora sets the microphone in the holder and looks directly at Garret. Their eyes lock for what feels like minutes, much longer than would be socially acceptable for people who don't know each other. In fact, everybody in the room notices her staring at him and they all turn to look at him. Garret's face gets even redder, if that's even possible, with the increased attention.

He stands and puts his napkin on his plate. "I'm gonna go to the bathroom and splash some cold water on my face."

"Do you think it was the food?" I ask, knowing full well it's not the food.

He shrugs. "Maybe. I don't know." He quickly turns around and walks towards the exit.

I look back at Kora, then to my retreating husband. I notice the guy next to me also staring at Garret as he's walking out of the room. He then looks at me and gives me a look of pity. I am filled with rage. I don't need his pity. I don't need anyone's pity.

I stare back at Garret's retreating form and the moment he rounds the corner, I look back at Kora. She's staring at the empty door, an expression of sadness on her face. What have you done, Garret? Whatever is going on between them is clearly serious. The look that was on both of their faces makes me believe that it was more than a crush.

All those months he spent in Los Angeles were always suspicious to me. It never made sense that he had to be there five days a week, for months on end. How could I be so stupid?

Kora takes a deep breath and continues her next song, remaining professional amid such an uncomfortable situation.

I look around the room. Everyone has gone back to their conversations and their meals, but I can't let go of the shock I feel. It's as if my entire world has just turned upside down. Garret's quick exit would be enough evidence of his guilt to anyone reasonable. I don't even know what to do with myself anymore.

I stare at my dessert, half-finished. I was so excited about it, but now my stomach is turning and I can't even fathom putting another bite in my mouth. I swore I wouldn't let Garret ruin this weekend, but I don't know if I can sit here anymore. It's too much.

Slowly, I rise from my seat and push the chair in. I glance at Kora one more time. Her eyes meet mine briefly. My hand still grasps my necklace, the one that is the same as hers. Tears briefly rise in Kora's eyes, but she blinks them away and then looks away from me. In the brief second that our eyes lock, a silent realization passes between us. We're in love with the same man.

15

AMELIA

I walk slowly away from the dining room, not exactly sure where to go. I don't really want to follow Garret. Right now, I don't even want to look at his face. What has he done to me? To us? He is destroying everything we've taken years to build and I am devastated. I slowly make my way back to our room, hoping that he's not there. As soon as I open the door, I can smell the alcohol before I even see him.

Garret is sitting on the bed, his tie undone, his shoes kicked off haphazardly on the floor. He's holding a bottle of alcohol in one hand that looks like it's nearly empty. Did he down all of that in the few moments he's been up here alone? He doesn't even glance at me as I come in, but just stares into space.

He takes another swig from his bottle as I close the door behind me. I walk up to the foot of the bed and stare at him, waiting for him to even acknowledge me. I stand there for what feels like at least ten minutes. He doesn't make any attempt to even look in my direction. It's as if I no longer even exist in his world.

I kick the bed. "Garret," I mutter.

His eyes slowly meet mine.

I continue, frustration evident in my voice. "Why did you leave?"

"I told you I wasn't feeling well," he replies.

"That's crap," I tell him. "You were fine until you saw that woman on stage."

He stares at me silently, taking another swig from the bottle. The golden liquid dribbles down his face. Great, he's somehow already at the sloppy drunk stage. I don't have much longer before he's incoherent.

"Did you know her, Garret?"

"Why would you even ask me that question?"

"Please, Garret, just be honest with me for once. Things haven't been right between us for years and I've had my suspicions about you cheating on me for a long time. It's not normal for a husband to spend five days a week in another city if he doesn't have to. There's no reason why you had to do all your business in Los Angeles. So yeah, of course, I've wondered if there was another woman. Is that her? Is she the one that you left me every week to go see?"

He glares at me, fire in his eyes. "Why did you pick this resort of all places, Amelia? We could have gone anywhere for our anniversary and you brought us here. Why?"

What is he trying to say? Is he trying to insinuate that I set this up? "Like I already told you, I found a special deal for it posted on social media. That's it. I thought it would be a good opportunity for us to get away together."

He laughs at me. "Right. You're telling me this is a complete coincidence? You're asking me to be honest with you and yet you're here, lying to my face. If you're not willing to be honest with me, like you're begging me to be with you, then we have nothing to talk about," he says.

"You never answered my question. Who is she?"

He just stares at me, venom in his eyes.

I'm tired of dancing around the subject, hoping he will do the right thing and confess. I just need to ask him point blank. I take a deep breath and find the courage deep down inside of me. Our eyes lock.

"Are you cheating on me, Garret? With her? Tell me the truth."

He stands from the bed and stumbles towards me, a look of hatred in his eyes. "I don't play games, Amelia. And this situation that you've set up is the worst kind of game. I'm not dealing with it."

Garret looks at his now-empty bottle, then walks over to the beverage cart. He grabs a wine bottle and a half-full bottle of scotch. He passes by me, his eyes glassy, but somehow still shooting daggers into my heart. He then leaves the hotel room without even glancing back at me.

I sit on the bed, devastated. He wouldn't even answer my question. Yet, I know deep down inside of me that what I accused him of was the truth.

Maybe I was foolish to think that a weekend away would be enough to convince him to choose me over whatever else he had going on, but I could have never predicted him to behave this way and so blatantly disregard me or my feelings.

I've known for years that something was going on, but I didn't have solid confirmation until this very moment. He didn't have to tell me directly for me to know. I saw the truth in his eyes the second he saw her. I think about the beautiful woman who was standing on stage. Why her? Why is the sight of her bothering him so much when I can't even get him to notice me?

I walk into the bathroom and remove my gown and my

makeup. All the work that I put in to restore myself to my previous glory was pointless. Garret didn't even see me. Not really. It's as if I am a ghost to him. Why do I even try?

I put on an oversized T-shirt and a pair of sweatpants. I grab a bottle of whiskey from the liquor cart and set it on the nightstand next to the bed. I crawl into it, allowing myself to sink into the soft pillows. I sit up and unscrew the lid on the bottle, taking a long drink and allowing the warm liquid to burn down my throat. A tear slides down my cheek and I swipe it away. I refuse to cry over this man. I've shed too many tears over the years, not tonight.

16

AMELIA

I race through the hallways of the unrenovated portion of the prison, following a tall, dark woman in the distance. She races away from me and disappears around the corner. I pick up my speed, trying to catch her, but as soon as I turn the corner myself, I see she's already at the end of the hallway, disappearing around another corner. She's going to get away.

"Wait!" I yell. My voice echoes down the empty hallway. "Come back!" I run as fast as I can to catch up with her, my sneakers squeaking on the polished linoleum floor as I run.

I get to the end of the hallway and look in the direction the woman ran. I am surprised to find her standing at the end of the hallway, staring in my direction and clutching the jade pendant hanging from her neck.

"Wait," I say breathlessly. "I just want to talk."

She hesitates, but doesn't move. I quickly move towards her, but before I can reach her, my hands cover my ears as a loud ringing noise blasts in the hallways. The figure of the woman begins to distort as if she's about to break apart because of the sound. The walls around me begin to dissolve. I try to brace myself against a part of the wall that still seems solid, but then it disintegrates also and I start to fall into the dark nothingness behind it.

SUDDENLY, I'm dragged from the depths of my dream by the unrelenting sound of the phone ringing. I slowly crack open my eyes and glance at my phone. It's only three a.m. Who's calling me at this hour?

I glance over at the other side of the bed. It's still perfectly made. Garret never slept in it. I grab the ringing phone and silence it by picking it up. My head is pounding and the last thing I need is to talk to someone. I glance at the nightstand and the now half-empty bottle of whiskey catches my eye. I don't even remember drinking that much. No wonder my head feels as if it's about to explode.

I take a deep breath and bring the phone to my ear. "Hello?" I say quietly.

"Mrs. Lawson, this is Miles at the front desk."

"Yes?" I ask, annoyed.

"There appear to be some power outages in the area because of the blizzard that's coming in. Our own power has flickered on and off several times over the last hour. If the power does go out for good, we do not have a way to heat the guest rooms."

I rub my eyes. "So, what does this mean?"

"Mostly, I'm just calling all the residents to assure them that no matter what happens, you will be safe. We have installed a large fireplace in the banquet hall; it also has its own heating system and generator. We're asking that you come down here for the night. You'll be warm here and safe if we were to lose power."

"Am I not safe in my room?"

"We're not quite sure what will happen to the doors to your room and the door to the wing that you're staying in if the power goes out. Several of the doors can be operated remotely and, therefore, have power running to them. If the power source fails, you may get locked inside your room; we're not sure. If you do, there's no heat... and... well... we don't want to take the risk to find out what would happen if there was no heat."

"Okay," I murmur. How could they build a resort and not put generators in every wing where guests were staying? Maybe Garret was right; they aren't really ready for people. Maybe this soft opening was just some way to recoup costs so they could finish building the resort. I feel stupid for even bringing us here.

I realize that Miles is still silently waiting for my response on the other end of the line. "Fine," I say reluctantly. "I'll come down."

"Please make sure to bring your husband too," Miles says. "We don't want anyone in their rooms when the power is out."

I have no idea where Garret is, but I don't want to tell Miles that after what happened earlier in the day. "Okay, we'll be there. Just give us a few moments," I say.

"There's no real rush. Take your time," Miles says, worry evident in his voice. It's clear that he's lying when he continues. "The storm isn't supposed to arrive for another hour, but they can be unpredictable at times, so I wouldn't take all night."

I look towards the empty side of the bed again. Where's Garret? He always just takes off when he's upset. We never get to resolve our issues like a normal couple. He leaves to cool down and by the time he comes back, he doesn't want to talk about whatever it was we were fighting about anymore. It's a vicious cycle.

I slowly crawl out of bed. As my feet hit the floor, the entire room starts to spin. I lay back down. I don't know if I can do this. Why did I drink that much? Now I have to figure out how to navigate through this hangover to the banquet hall by myself. If Garret were here, I could at least hold his arm and use him as support.

I try again, putting my feet on the ground and standing slowly. The room starts to spin again, but I hold my ground until the spinning lessens and I can move forward. I open my suitcase and grab a pair of yoga pants along with a large, oversized sweater. If I'm going to be forced to hang out with the rest of the guests, I'm going to be comfortable.

I think about leaving Garret a note, but then think better of it. I don't need to always be his keeper. If he gets to the room and can't find me, he can always text me. Although, there's a chance my phone won't be working. You know what? Screw him. He can just come look for me the way I looked for him earlier. Maybe he'll even get stuck in the snow like I did. I shouldn't have to always be the one doing the hunting.

I grab my coat and a pair of boots, just in case and slip them on. I notice the camera I bought Garret for his birthday lying on the nightstand next to the bed. I must have set it there when I came back to the room. I quickly grab it and shove it into my bag. This thing cost me more than I'd like to admit; I can't just leave it here to be stolen. Besides, I've never seen a real blizzard before. Maybe I can take some photographs when the sun comes up again.

I open the door and enter the great room. I see couples walking hand in hand out of the rooms and down the stairs. A pang of guilt and sadness hits me, replacing my earlier resolve to leave Garret in the lurch. If we were to change places, I would want him to communicate with me. I grab my phone and send him a quick message. I still have service, so hopefully, he'll get it.

As I walk to the banquet hall, following behind the other guests, my thoughts are clouded with worry. Maybe he's already in the hall waiting for me and I'll realize all of this worry was for nothing. I try to convince myself that everything is fine and I'm simply being plagued by an overactive imagination.

I hold onto a sliver of hope that we can find each other again, both literally and figuratively. If we get through this morning, then we only have one more night at this resort. However, if the rest of our time goes the way last night did, our relationship is doomed to fail.

I arrive at the banquet hall and scan the room. No sign of Garret. Where the heck did he go?

17

AMELIA

The banquet hall is dimly lit. The overhead lights are not at full power. Instead, they glow a soft orange color as if they're trying to conserve electricity. The windows to the outside barely let in any light as the impending blizzard blocks out the stars and the moon. The wind howls through the trees, causing them to bend as if they were made of something soft and pliable and not solid wood. Snow dances in the wind, making several twists and turns before eventually falling into a soft layer on the already white ground.

I scan the room one more time, looking for Garret, but he's nowhere to be found. I slowly make my way to a group of couches in the corner of the room. I don't remember couches being here last night when we had dinner, but I was a little distracted, so maybe I just didn't notice.

My head pounds from having had too much to drink and my vision is blurred. I'm not sure if it's from a lack of sleep or a headache. Either way, it makes it difficult for me to move forward in a straight line.

I eventually make it to the couches and I find an empty

seat across from a couple who seem madly in love. They are wrapped in each other's arms under a blanket, whispering sweet words to each other. I don't even want to know what they're doing under that blanket.

I shake my head. I want to be happy for them, but there's a voice inside of me that just wants to scream at them. It's never going to last. They're happy now, but just wait to see what the years do. There's a part of me that feels they need to know the truth. I stop myself, of course. Maybe it's not like this for everyone. Maybe some couples remain blissfully happy through several decades of marriage, instead of basically hating each other.

Suddenly, a squealing noise echoes through the large room as Miles turns on an amp and speaker to project his voice using a mic. The screeching subsides and Miles clears his throat. "Excuse me, everyone. May I have your attention, please?"

We all shift in our chairs and turn towards him, giving him our undivided attention.

He speaks into the mic. "As I have mentioned to most of the people here, there's a blizzard coming. These do happen frequently in the mountains and for the most part, they are nothing to worry about. We've asked you all to come here because as of now, this is the only place in the resort that has a generator. So far, the furnace seems to be working in this room and the power is still on, but in case the power goes out, we do not want you guys in your rooms without light or heat."

I look around the room and count how many people are here. Aside from a few staff, there are only twelve, a total of six couples. Did the rest of the staff leave after dinner? Is this all of the guests this weekend? What kind of grand opening event only has six couples attend? I begin to wonder if Garret had been right. Maybe we are test subjects for the resort, so they can work out all the kinks and the details before they actually open to the public. This isn't a special weekend or a grand opening of any kind; this is just a trial run and we're the guinea pigs.

I keep my eye on the doors, hoping that Garret will walk in at any moment. What if he's with her? The woman who caused him to be a red-faced, blubbering idiot last night and invaded my dreams this morning. I can't believe she's the one he's been cheating on me with the entire time. Who knows how many women there were, honestly? She's probably just the most recent recruit on a whole roster.

The jade necklace she was wearing last night was like a bright green sign. What would be the chance of it being a coincidence that we both had the exact same necklace? I shake my head — almost zero.

I look around and find that the singer is missing too. What if they're together? What if they're having an affair right under my nose in the same hotel? The thought of it makes me sick to my stomach. I can put up with a lot, but that kind of betrayal is something I can't stomach.

I focus back on the conversation Miles is having with the small crowd. He's answering people's questions. Many of them sound more worried about being stuck here for longer than the weekend than they are worried about their own safety.

A blonde woman raises her hand. "I have a very important hair appointment on Monday that I cannot miss. I've been waiting to see this stylist for months now. How are you going to ensure that I get home?"

Miles keeps his composure as he answers the question. "We have four-wheel-drive vehicles along with chains for the tires. As long as the blizzard stops, we can assure you that you will get home on time, but if there is still a blizzard going come Monday morning, I will not be risking the lives of my employees just so you can get your hair done, ma'am."

She crosses her arms, clearly annoyed by his response. Her husband smirks as he watches her pout, but the smirk doesn't last for long before he takes her in his arms and comforts her. Even that childish woman has a better relationship with her partner than I do.

I shake my head. Maybe I should go find Garret, but as soon as I say this, the snow flurries pick up outside and the lights flash again. After several seconds of them flickering off and on, all the lights outside of the banquet hall go out.

18

AMELIA

The crowd is murmuring, drowning out Miles's attempts to calm everyone down. I can tell several of them are worried, but some are just plain angry.

"Excuse me," Miles says into the microphone. "Can I please have your attention?"

The talking stops slowly as Miles continues to ask for attention. Eventually, everyone is silent and we all turn our eyes back to Miles. "There's another issue I need to discuss with you all. One much more severe than this blizzard and the power outage."

Silence blankets the room as we all wait in anticipation of his announcement. "The singer that you all heard last night at dinner, Kora Mendez, was found dead in her room."

Loud gasps erupt throughout the room, followed by a cacophony of voices. Miles gives everyone a few minutes to react. I just sit and stare, watching all of them in stunned silence. The woman Garret followed down that hallway is dead? It's obvious that he knew her and his behavior has been suspicious since we got here. Are people going to think he had something to do with her death?

Suddenly, I feel a tap on my shoulder. Startled, I look up. "Garret, what the heck? Where have you been?"

"What's going on?" He asks.

I don't even want to tell him. He's been MIA for hours now and comes in as if nothing has happened. I nod towards Miles, but keep my mouth shut. If I start talking to him now, who knows where the conversation will lead? That's definitely not a conversation I want to have in public.

Garret and I listen as Miles taps on the mic one more time to get everyone's attention. The blonde woman from before raises her hand. "What happened to her? She didn't look sick or anything last night."

"I'm not exactly sure. We can't rule out foul play, but it could have been anything. We don't know yet," Miles responds.

Garret leans over to me. "What are they talking about?" He asks, concerned.

"Shhh. Just listen," I say dismissively. I'm not going to be the one to tell him his girlfriend is dead.

A man across the room raises his hand and speaks up. "Who would do something like that? What makes you think it was foul play?"

Miles holds up both of his hands. "I didn't say that exactly. I'm just saying that from what we think we know, she was healthy and young."

The crowd starts murmuring once again.

I glance over at Garret. His arms are crossed and his face is unreadable. His eyes, however, tell the story. He's devastated and trying to hide it from everyone. While he didn't admit that he was having an affair with her, it's pretty obvious. I can't remember the last time he's shown any kind of emotion like this. He's usually really good at hiding what he's feeling deep down inside of him, but now, the tears forming in his eyes are solid evidence of his grief.

A loud tapping sound can be heard over the speakers. I look up; Miles is tapping on the microphone with his hand, trying to get everybody's attention once more. "As I was saying, we are taking precautions. While the storm was the main reason we had you all come here, we also want to contain everybody in one location while we investigate the circumstances. We want to make sure that nobody goes anywhere until the authorities come here and do their official investigation. That won't happen until the blizzard passes," Miles explains.

He points towards one of the other couples present — a tall, dark-haired man and his elegant-looking wife. "Dr. Dina Callaway and her husband Pat have been guests with us since before Kora arrived at the resort."

Dr. Callaway raises her hand and looks around the room.

Miles continues. "Dr. Callaway graciously agreed to examine the body and confirmed that Kora is no longer with us. She was not able to tell if it was the result of foul play; that part is still unknown. Now, we just have to wait until the police can get here to do a thorough investigation."

The blonde woman raises her hand once again. "We really can't go back to our rooms?"

Miles hesitates. "Obviously, I can't hold you hostage. This is no longer a real prison and I am not a warden, but we ask that you remain here for the time being until we know what happened and who did this."

A brown-haired woman looks towards the blonde-haired woman. "Anyone who leaves is going to look suspicious, you know that, right?"

The blonde-haired woman crosses her arms and sinks back in her chair in a childish pout.

"Exactly," Miles says. "We want to make sure that all of you walk away from here without any rumors or anyone being falsely accused of her death." His voice cracks in the middle of his words and I can tell he's also trying to keep his composure. What was it about this woman that these men are so upset over her?

Miles continues. "We ask, for the foreseeable future, that you remain here. We will keep you comfortable, make sure you have plenty of food and water and provide warm blankets and pillows."

"I didn't pay for this resort to be sleeping on a couch," the man across the room yells.

"I understand, sir. And we will discuss reimbursing you some of your fees," Miles responds.

The man crosses his arms and looks sourly at Miles.

I look towards Garret, our eyes lock and in that brief exchange, so much is communicated between us. Is that fear I see in his eyes, or maybe an apology? I'm not sure, but what I do know is that the secrets that he has been trying so desperately to hide are about to be fully exposed and he's terrified.

I look out the window. The visibility is low as snow swirls in the air. I'm not sure I'm ready for what's about to happen.

19

AMELIA

As the guests discuss the news of Kora's death, the noise in the banquet hall rises from a general murmur to a small roar. Fear and uncertainty hang in the air. Some of the couples attempt to use their cell phones, only to find there's no reception. The cell phone towers must have been damaged in the storm. Panic starts to grip the room as we all begin to realize the gravity of the situation.

Garret and I sit on the couch, not talking. Honestly, I don't even know what there is to say to him. He's clearly distraught by this situation. He had a whole life that I knew pretty much nothing about and the thought of that makes me sick to my stomach. My mind is racing through all the events of the last few years, trying to contemplate what exactly went wrong. How did we end up in this position? We are sitting here at a resort, contemplating the murder of my husband's mistress. I couldn't make this up if I tried.

I peek over at Garret. His expression is unchanged. His jaw is still clenched and his face is a sickly pale white. His eyes still tell the same story they did earlier; he is breaking up inside. I feel like I'm a million miles away, like an observer looking in on his life from the outside through shattered glass. I can't even reach him or help him in any way. This is a pain of his own making and he's going to have to go through it alone.

Suddenly, a loud noise erupts from the other side of the room and I turn to see the doctor's husband, Pat, angrily walking towards us. His face is filled with fury. "You knew her," he says, pointing at Garret.

Fear washes over Garret's face, immediately replaced by the hardness that was there before. He stands. "I don't know what you're talking about. You don't know me. Do you even know my name?"

Pat ignores the question. "I saw you last night. You and Kora locked eyes for a long time during her performance and then you left. You knew her," Pat accuses.

The room falls silent. I can feel everybody's eyes on us. How many more people noticed the connection between Kora and Garret last night?

"That's right. They locked eyes and then he left," the blonde woman pipes up. "I saw it too."

Garret crosses his arms. "I wasn't feeling very well. Something in the food didn't sit right with me and I had to go to the bathroom, if you must know."

"Right, likely story," Pat says. "You looked like you were trying to run away."

Pat is directly in front of Garret's face, his finger merely inches from his nose. As he speaks, angry spittle spews out of his mouth, blanketing Garret's face in a fine film. Garret wipes off his face with his hand and tries to back up, but stumbles into the couch, unable to go any further. Instead of pushing past him, he stands his ground, staring at Pat with contempt in his eyes.

Miles, desperate to keep an altercation from occurring, forces his way between the two men. He puts one hand on both of their chests and pushes them aside and away from each other. "Back up, guys. Back up," he says. "Let's not make this any worse than it already is."

Pat reluctantly backs up, creating space between him and Garret.

When Miles is assured that Pat isn't going to attack him, he turns to Garret. "Did you know Kora?"

"No, no, I didn't know her," Garret says defensively.

"Where did you go last night and why were you late today?" Miles asks.

"Like I told you, I've been feeling sick," Garret says. "Ever since dinner last night, I've been laying in bed this whole time, unable to move."

Garret glances at me, pleading with his eyes. I look away, disgusted by him, but unwilling to speak up and out him to this group of strangers. He's still my husband. If he did this, we can wait for the police to investigate. He doesn't need to be attacked by an angry mob. I keep my mouth shut. Silence is all I'm willing to give.

"Just ask my wife," he says, pointing at me.

How dare he put me on the spot like this? Silence was one thing, but now he wants me to vouch for him? Not only is he unwilling to tell me what happened between him and Kora or who she was to him, but now he wants me to lie for him outright.

I shoot daggers at him. Why would he put me in this position? All eyes are on me and the pressure I feel is too much to bear. I have to say something to get them to back off. Maybe I can get away with saying just enough of the truth to make them believe I'm validating his story.

"He was sick last night and he's been sick ever since," I

say. Little do they know that it's been heartsickness he's been dealing with, not some reaction to the food.

"See," Miles says, "this is not worth our time. Please, everybody, go back to your seats."

I glare at Garret. As soon as everyone is far enough away, I walk over to him and whisper in his ear. "What have you done?"

"Nothing. I swear. I know it looks bad, but I've done nothing."

"Who was she to you, Garret?"

Instead of responding, he stares down at the camera lying on my hip. "Why did you bring that?"

Taken aback by his question, I answer defensively. "It cost me too much money just to leave it in the room and there's no way it would fit in the tiny safe, so I just grabbed it." Then it dawns on me; he's just deflecting. "Answer my question, Garret. Who is she to you?"

He stares at me in silence. The weight of it hangs heavy between us.

I continue. "Your silence tells me everything. How long have you been sleeping with her?"

"Please," he begs. "Not now. Not here."

"You just asked me to lie for you, but you won't give me the truth?"

"I promise I'll tell you everything. As soon as this is all over."

I stare into his eyes for a long time and find nothing but grief and fear — no guilt, no remorse, nothing. Only fear for no one but himself. He makes me sick.

"Whatever, Garret. You don't care about me. You don't care about us. I don't think you have for a really long time."

"But I do," he pleads. "I promise I do."

"Then prove it."

20

AMELIA

The guests and the staff mingle in clusters, each group whispering to each other about what happened to Kora, speculating about the truth and developing wild stories to fit their beliefs. Accusations and speculations run rampant.

In the beginning, Miles makes his way from group to group in an attempt to calm them down, but it's not working. After several minutes, he makes his way back up to the microphone and taps it to get everybody's attention. A loud screeching sound erupts from the speaker. The talking stops and everyone's hands raise to protect their ears.

Miles quickly adjusts something on the speaker that stops the screeching sound. Everyone lowers their hands. "Please, everyone, calm down," he says into the mic. "As I was walking around the room, I heard dozens of speculations about what happened to Kora. The truth is, we don't even know if it's foul play. Yes, Dr. Callaway confirmed that she's no longer with us, but the room was too dark because of the generator situation, so she wasn't able to get a really definitive look at her."

"Well, then fix the generator," a voice yells from the crowd.

Miles holds up his hands defensively. "Believe me, I've been trying. This room is the only room in the complex that is fully powered. The rest of the rooms are dimly lit and cold. From what I understand, that generator is supposed to be able to power everything in this building, including the rooms, so I'm not sure what's going on with it."

Miles looks dejected for several seconds as he contemplates the situation and then his face lights up. "Maybe one of you could help. Is there anyone here with experience with generators or even someone with tech experience?"

I know I should raise my hand, but I hesitate. One of the things that most people don't know about me is that I grew up in the backwoods of Montana. My immediate family are what you would call preppers; they stockpile everything from canned goods to firewood and weapons, preparing themselves for the potential end of the world. Every single one of the houses around my parent's house has a solar-powered generator. For many of the families, the generator costs more than their cars.

My dad wanted us to be prepared for any eventuality. He taught me how to use and repair our generator in the chance that something happened to him and he wasn't able to be here to take care of it himself. He wanted to make sure that we would always be safe. I wasn't the oldest, but I was the most like him and I guess he trusted me with the responsibility. Eventually, I moved from hardware to software, but that's how I got my start with tech. That background is also the reason the VP at NextGen was so impressed with me. I guess it was just a different story than her Ivy League subordinates.

I don't readily share this information with others. I have

always been embarrassed by my parents, especially as a teenager. We would go to the grocery store in the main town near us and my dad would fill the cart with at least a hundred cans of green beans, especially when they were on sale. The following week, it would be one hundred cans of something else. The clerk and the customers would always give us the weirdest looks, like they thought we were crazy. I just wanted them to stop looking.

I never got that wish. I think my parents got even crazier as I got older, or maybe I just became more aware of how insane their ways were. When I left home at eighteen, I went in the complete opposite direction of the simple country life. I got a degree in IT and worked as a computer programmer for a few years at a large corporation. After taking time off because of my first miscarriage, I tried to go back, but I couldn't handle the looks of pity.

No one meant any harm, but it only highlighted my body failing me. It didn't help that nearly everyone there was a man. At times, I think they felt more bad for me than my own husband did. Two more miscarriages later and I got the courtesy clerk gig at the grocery store. I tried so hard to leave behind the simple life; it's so interesting how when things got hard, it was the place I felt the most safe.

My parents never really understood why I tried to embrace everything they were against. When I would come home from college on breaks, they would grill me about my choices and make me feel terrible. After a few years, I realized I loved my parents, but I couldn't be around them anymore. I had to distance myself from their all-encompassing views of the world and their incessant criticism of me.

I didn't exactly keep my promise. Up until a few years ago, I went home probably once a year to visit them. Each time I did, it didn't take long before I just wanted to leave and never come back. While it was always nice to hug my parents, I couldn't handle being around the constant fear that they lived in; it wasn't good for my mental health.

Eventually, my visits to see my family grew less and less. We would talk on the phone occasionally, but I haven't made the trip to Montana in a couple of years. While I've kept up a relationship with my sister Marigold, my relationship with my parents and the rest of my siblings is almost non-existent these days.

Besides, my parents have never really liked Garret. "He's always hiding something," my mom would always say to me. "You be careful. I don't trust him."

I never believed her, just always chalked it up to one of her paranoid ideas. Now, I think maybe she had more wisdom than I realized.

Miles is asking for volunteers to help him work on the generator for a second time. "Maybe there's someone here that doesn't have a full-blown career in computer programming or working with generators, but has dabbled in it? Anything would be better than my skills. I barely know how to plug in the coffee machine in the mornings."

Nervous laughter erupts from the small crowd.

I hesitate and then slowly raise my hand. I speak up over the crowd as soon as Miles notices me. "I have some experience with generators and I used to work in IT. I might be able to help."

Garret looks at me and his jaw drops.

"That would be amazing," Miles says. "Amelia, you come with me. The rest of you, just stay here and wait for the blizzard to stop and the authorities to come. Please try to remain calm."

Garret grabs my elbow and whispers in my ear. "What are you doing, Amelia?" He hisses.

I yank my elbow away from his grasp. "What do you care, Garret? I'm just trying to help."

"For all you know, Miles could be the killer. I'm not letting you go off with him by yourself. I'm going with you."

I glare at him. "You really think Miles's the one who did this? You know everybody in here thinks it was you."

"I swear I did nothing to Kora. Nothing," he insists.

An angry voice rises above the rest of the conversations happening across the room. I look over and see Pat staring straight at Garret. "You can't leave if you're the prime suspect. We'd be crazy just to let you waltz out of here. No way."

The rest of the crowd nods in agreement.

I whisper to Garret through my teeth. "I'll be fine. Besides, I feel just as safe going with Miles as I do being here with you right now."

"What's that supposed to mean?" He asks.

"Just that I have no idea who you are or what you're capable of right now and that makes me feel unsafe."

Suddenly, I feel a tap on my shoulder. I turn around to see one of the chefs standing there, still wearing her chef's uniform and hat. "I couldn't help but overhear you two and I agree with your husband. You should not go with Miles by yourself. Don't get me wrong, Miles is a great guy, but until we know more, it's not safe to trust anyone. I will go with you," she says.

Garret looks at her and nods. "Fine," he says. "At least you two won't be alone."

I shake my head. "You're ridiculous," I say. "Like you have any right to tell me what to do at this point. We came here for us and you've spent most of it who knows where, with who knows who. And now you think you have the right to pretend to care about me? You're a fool," I tell him.

Miles walks over to us and interrupts before Garret can respond. "Thank you so much for volunteering, Amelia."

"Of course," I say, pointing to the chef, not quite sure of her name. "Miss..."

"Sarah," she says, saving me from embarrassment.

"Right, Sarah has agreed to go with us so that we are not in pairs. It's just for added protection, you know?"

"That is a great idea," Miles says. "In fact, I think everybody should operate like that until the authorities come."

He walks back up to the mic. "Excuse me, one last time, please. If anyone needs to go to the bathroom, you should all travel in threes for safety reasons. We still have no idea what happened to Kora and if it was foul play, it had to have been one of us. I don't want anyone else to be hurt."

Garret crosses his arms in silent protest as Miles, Sarah and I exit the room and head towards the generator.

21

GARRET

I watch Amelia disappear through the door towards the generator and I suddenly feel very alone. I sit on the couch and stare at the blizzard going on outside. For some reason, it almost seems more inviting than my current situation. How did things end up such a mess? And what the heck happened to Kora? I loved her. I won't say I loved her more than I once loved Amelia, but it was different.

Ever since Amelia and I got married, I felt a sense of obligation to her. Yes, I loved her, but it was the type of love you chose, not the kind of love that happens to you like an unstoppable train. I knew that she would be a good partner and a good mother someday and those qualities were what attracted me to her. I knew my life would be good if I chose her as my wife.

In the beginning, there was a small spark between us, but especially after the miscarriages, that spark completely disappeared. I don't blame her at all; it is just our reality now. For years, we've been operating more as business partners and friends than lovers.

When I met Kora, there was just something about her

that took my breath away. She electrified my life in a way that's never happened before. My love for her was passionate and reckless. I felt alive when I was with her, like she had somehow raised me from the dead.

What was she even doing here at this resort? How did Amelia and I end up here, in the same place that Kora is performing? And now she's dead. The situation is just so strange and surreal and now I have to hide my grief because everyone will use it against me.

A presence lingers over me. I look up. Pat is standing there, accusation glaring from his eyes. "Tell me how you knew her," he says.

I put up my hands. My only safe way out of this is just to lie. "I don't know what you're talking about. Like I said before, I didn't know her."

"None of us believes that. There was a clear connection between the two of you at dinner last night. Everybody saw it."

"I don't know what to tell you, man. I've never seen her before in my life."

Behind Pat stands two other couples. Pat's wife is nowhere to be found, but the blonde-haired girl and her husband and another couple, stand there with their arms crossed as if they are the judge, jury and executioner.

"Okay, fine. Let's say you were sick last night," Pat says. "Where were you this morning? Most of us got in this room way before you. Don't you agree that looks pretty suspicious?"

"I get why it looks suspicious, but I promise I did not hurt Kora. I was feeling so bad; it just took me a while to leave our room. I didn't come out until I was so cold in the room that I couldn't stand it anymore. That's it. Just ask my wife. She was there with me."

Deep down, I hope that Amelia will continue to lie for me. She did it once before she left, but I'm not sure if she has it in her to do it again. If she doesn't, my entire life might explode.

Pat glares at me, clearly not buying my excuses. It's obvious I'm on thin ice here. These people have already tried and convicted me in their hearts and minds. I hate the fact that I have to lie about where I was, but if I tell them the truth, then they're really going to think that I'm guilty. "Please, man, just go back over there. I'll talk to the cops when they get here. I won't leave this room, I promise. Just please, leave me alone," I plead.

Pat crosses his arms, contemplating my words. After several seconds, he nods once. "Come on, guys. He's not going to give us anything. We'll just keep our eyes on him," he says.

With that, they all walk back toward their seats. I notice that the other guests are lying down on the couches, many of them snuggled in their partner's arms.

I shake my head. I haven't been close to Amelia like that in years. To be honest, I didn't even really give this weekend a chance. I came mostly to appease her and to make it look like I was trying. I had no real intentions of trying to fix things between me and her. I've had one foot in and one foot out for years.

So often, I dream of a life in which I'm in a loving relationship with a woman who adores me. When I saw Kora walking down that hallway yesterday, I thought maybe this was my chance to win her back. I had no idea what was going to happen later.

22

KORA (PAST)

Norma went back home to visit her family, so Garret and I have the apartment to ourselves this week. Let's just say we've been taking full advantage of it. I think we've hooked up in almost every room in the apartment.

Tonight, we've decided to take it easy and Garret is cooking dinner for me.

"It smells amazing in here," I say as I walk into the kitchen. Garret is standing in front of the stove, tending a pot of boiling water. "What are you making?" I ask as I walk behind him and wrap my arms around him.

He stops stirring and turns around towards me, putting his arms around my neck. "I can't cook a lot of things," he says, "but I am the master at making fettuccine Alfredo."

"Really?" I ask. "Just like you were the master of making pancakes?" I tease, a smile spreading on my lips.

"That's not fair," he says in mock hurt. "I promise, this is my specialty."

"I can't wait," I say seriously.

Suddenly, I hear the sound of water sizzling on the cooktop. “Garret...” I exclaim.

He quickly turns back towards the stove to deal with the overflow.

“I’m just going to sit over here and stay out of your way,” I say.

He looks at me, embarrassed. “I promise, I’m good at this. You’re just so distracting.”

I laugh. “You don’t mind this kind of distraction, do you?”

“Not at all, but we might end up with some burnt food.”

I grab a bottle of wine and a couple of glasses out of the cabinet before sitting at the table. I uncork the wine and pour us both a glass. “Here,” I tell him, “I find that sometimes a glass of wine helps things go more smoothly when you’re cooking.”

“That’s surprising coming from you,” he says, grabbing the glass and downing it in almost one gulp.

I giggle. “Well, sipping on occasion is fine, but I don’t think chugging was necessary.”

“It was, trust me.”

I watch him cook in silence until the meal is prepared. I can’t believe how lucky I am. I’ve never been more in love with a person in my entire life. He just gets me. He understands my goals and my ambitions. He encourages me to be the person I’m supposed to be. I want more than just Monday through Friday. I want him here all the time.

He sets the plates down in front of us. The pasta looks delicious. “Dig in,” he says.

I swirl my fork in the noodles and take a huge bite. It is creamy and rich, much better than I ever expected it to be. “Wow,” I say as soon as I swallow. “This is the best fettuccine Alfredo I’ve ever had.”

"Told you so," he says. "Have I redeemed myself from that pancake disaster?"

"And then some," I say. "You can make this for me every night if you want to. Of course, I might be five hundred pounds by the end of it, but man, it would be amazing."

He chuckles. "I'll definitely cook for you more often. I need to add a few more dinner dishes to my repertoire. This is about all I know how to make."

"Well, it's perfect," I say.

We eat in silence for several minutes as I gather up the courage to say what's really on my mind. I down my glass of wine and pour myself another. I drink half of that glass before finally speaking. "Garret, I've been meaning to ask you about something."

"Yeah?" He asks, his mouth full of food. "What is it?"

"What we have has been so incredible. I never want you to leave. When Fridays come and you fly back home, my heart breaks a little every time." I take a deep breath and continue. "Move in with me, Garret. Stay here every night."

"I don't know, Kora. I've put down so many roots in Las Vegas. It'd be difficult to leave them all behind."

I chuckle. "You make it sound like you've got a family there or something."

His face turns beet red and he just stares at me.

"What? Wait. You're joking, right?"

He stares at me, remorse in his eyes and shakes his head. "I'm not joking," he whispers.

"Are you... I mean, it's not like you're married, right?" I ask in a whisper, my voice tinged with disbelief and hurt.

"I am. I'm married." He nods.

The revelation hangs in the air between us like a dark cloud. I should have known better. I should have been more discerning. Of course, he's married. Why else would he have to go back every single weekend? He has not spent one weekend with me and now I understand why. It all makes perfect sense.

I continue. "Do you have kids?"

"No, not that I know of."

"No, Garret. This is not a joke. How could you do this to me, or to your wife? Are you separated or..."

Garret stares at me; his expression is a mixture of regret and frustration. He runs a hand through his hair, his eyes avoiding mine. "Kora, I... I didn't think you took us that seriously," he admits, his voice heavy with guilt. "I thought we were just having fun. I never would have guessed you were serious enough to want me to move in."

My gaze narrows and I can feel a surge of anger rising within me. "You didn't think I took us seriously?" I repeat incredulously. "Garret, we've been seeing each other for months. How could you not think I took this seriously? I'm not seeing anybody else besides you. What did you expect?"

"I don't know. I guess I just hoped I'd figure out the whole situation with my wife before we took the next step. I thought I had more time."

"You've been lying to me for months." The feeling of betrayal courses through my body. "I can't believe that I let myself think we had something special."

"We do," he says. "I love you, Kora. I am stuck in a loveless marriage. I haven't loved my wife in years. The only reason I've stayed has been because we have a fifty-fifty prenup, but now I don't care. I think I could possibly walk away now to be with you and it wouldn't affect us too much."

"Are you insane?" I ask, shocked. "What kind of man really thinks a woman is okay with being a mistress? The second option?"

"No, I didn't mean it like that, but I want to walk away from her. I want to be with you."

My shoulders slump. "I would have never even suggested you move here if I had known. I could never knowingly be the reason for all these lies."

"I understand. I'm sorry. Look, maybe you could move to Vegas with me," he suggests. "You'd be able to get a gig there."

I stare at him as tears fill my eyes. "I might have been willing to do that before, but you've lied to me for so long. I don't even know if I can trust you."

He looks at me, his eyes filled with remorse. "Kora, I never meant to hurt you," he says, his voice softer now. "I messed up. I'm so sorry."

The tears that were welling in my eyes begin to tip over and fall down my cheeks. "Sorry isn't enough, Garret," my voice wavers with emotion. "I deserve better than this. Your wife deserves better than this."

I realize at that moment that I have to walk away. I take another large drink of my wine as the reality of it all falls on me like a heavy blanket. I look up at Garret; his brows are scrunched in frustration. He places his head in his hands and rubs his temples.

"I can't do this anymore," I say quietly. "I think we have to end things."

He looks up at me quickly. "No, you can't mean that."

"I do. When we started dinner tonight, I wanted you to move in with me, but that was before I knew the entire truth. I'm not going to be a homewrecker. You could have saved us both the heartache and told me all of this from the beginning," I say.

He groans. "I know, I should have, but I was scared. I

wanted you to like me. I wanted you to hang out with me. And if I had told you that I was married, would you have?"

I shrug my shoulders. "Probably not, but either way, everyone would have been better off had you told me the truth." I take a deep breath, wipe the tears away from my face and stand. "I'm going to bed. You need to be out of here by morning. I don't want to see you again."

As I walk away from him, I can't help but feel utterly destroyed. I fell in love with him. I was beginning to hope that he was my forever person, but all of those hopes have been dashed in just a matter of a few minutes. I feel so stupid. Why did I just justify all of the red flags? Why didn't I investigate further why he wasn't here on weekends? I just accepted his answers. I believed him and now I look like a fool.

23

KORA (PAST)

"Do you guys want to take it again from the top?" I ask, looking towards my band.

The drummer looks towards me. "Yeah, but can we take a five-minute break? I gotta use the john."

I nod and step down from the stage. We're performing at one of our regular places, an upscale bar in the middle of Hollywood. I walk up to the bartender. "Can I have a gin and tonic, please?"

"Of course," he says. "You guys sound great."

"Thanks, we've been working really hard trying to fine-tune our set, hoping that someday somebody will walk in this place and discover us," I laugh.

"Good luck with that," he says. "Isn't that everybody's dream?"

"Right. At least I'm singing again. Before this last year, I hadn't sung in almost a decade."

"What?" He asks. "You're amazing, though."

"Yeah, I lost my way there for a bit, before someone I knew reminded me of who I was." The thought of Garret still stings. It feels like a piece of me has been ripped out of my chest. I haven't seen or talked to him for weeks, but I think about him every day.

Maybe I made a mistake. Maybe I should have given him a chance to make a space for me in his life. I've been trying desperately to piece my heart back together since he left, but it still feels like there's a hole inside my heart and I wonder if it will never be filled.

The waiter hands me my gin and tonic and I take a big gulp, downing the thing in a few seconds.

"Dang," he says. "You want another?"

I shake my head. "I better not. One's enough to give me liquid courage, two and I'll just be sloppy."

He laughs. "Makes sense. At least you know that about yourself. Lots of people have no idea what they're like after a couple of drinks."

"Trust me, I've learned the hard way," I say.

I walk back towards the stage and resume my position in front of the mic. The drummer returns and we begin rehearsing our song. Halfway through, a figure catches my eye, standing in the back of the bar. It's dark, so I can't quite see who it is right away, but as he walks forward and comes into the light, I stop singing in the middle of the chorus and openly stare.

"Everything okay?" the bass guitarist asks.

"I need a few minutes, guys. Sorry," I say as I set the mic down and walk quickly towards him. I stop a few feet away. He stands and stares at me, a hopeful look on his face.

"What are you doing here, Garret?" I ask.

"I came to see you," he says.

"I said I didn't want to see you again."

"I know, but I had to take a chance," he says. "Ever since

the day we broke up, I haven't been able to stop thinking about you, Kora. I didn't realize how much I loved you and how much I wanted you in my life."

"What about your wife?" I ask.

"I think I have a solution. Can we talk?" He asks.

I nod. "I don't have a lot of time. We have to keep rehearsing and we're on stage in an hour."

"Just give me ten minutes; that's all I need. I promise."

"Okay," I say hesitantly. I'm not sure I should give him a chance to work his way back into my life, but I'm curious about what he has to say.

We walk towards a booth in the back of the bar and sit across from each other. He reaches out and grabs my hand. I think about pulling it away, but I've missed him so much that I don't.

"What's your plan, Garret?"

"I'm going to leave my wife."

"That doesn't solve anything," I say.

He nods. "I've been setting the money up so both of us will come out fair. I'll get a divorce and I want you to come live with me in Vegas."

Hope springs in my chest, but I try to temper it. "I thought fifty-fifty *was* fair."

"The situation with my parents is complicated, but they wouldn't be too pleased with the prior arrangement."

"So you're rich-rich, basically?" I say it more as a statement than a question.

"I guess you can say my family is," he says. "But don't worry about that. Will you come to Vegas with me?"

"Do you mean that? What about my singing career? Are there even agents in Las Vegas? I don't know how that city works. There's a chance that I could never make it if I move there."

"You keep your gigs here. I'll fly you back to L.A. every weekend and I'll come see you for your gigs. We can make it work."

I stare at him for a long time before responding. "I refuse to be the other woman, Garret. I'm not going to be with you again until you are no longer with your wife. It's not fair to her and it's not fair to me."

"I understand. I'm going to do it soon, I promise. I just needed to know if you would be willing to make the move to be with me before I blew my life up like that."

There's a part of me that knows I should say no. He lied to me once and who's to say he's not going to lie to me again? Besides, marriages that are born out of affairs never end up well, but I still love him and I know deep down that I can't walk away. "Okay, I'll move," I say quietly.

Relief floods his face. "You have no idea how happy that makes me. I have something for you." He reaches into his pocket and pulls out a black jewelry box. He puts it on the table and slides it towards me.

I open it and gasp. Inside is a large jade pendant hung expertly on a silver chain. "It's beautiful," I say. "This must have cost you a fortune."

He shakes his head dismissively. "Don't worry about that. You deserve every bit of it. Can I put it on you?" He asks.

I nod and scoot over in the booth, making room for him to sit next to me. When he does, the electricity between us is palpable. I turn around and lift my hair. He reaches around my neck, lays the pendant on my chest and clasps it behind me. I turn back towards him.

"What do you think?" I ask.

"Gorgeous," he says, staring me in the eyes, not even looking at the necklace.

He draws me in close and our lips lock. Before the kiss becomes too passionate, I push him away. "I can't do this until I know for sure I'm not the other woman."

"I love you, Kora. I promise you, things are going to work out."

"I hope so, because I love you too."

24

GARRET (PAST)

As soon as I enter through the creaking wood door, I'm greeted with the scent of cedar wood and beer. Laughter erupts in the middle of the room, where a nearby group of friends huddle together, taking turns throwing hatchets at the wooden targets set at the far end of short lanes. Cheers erupt as one of them lands a bull's-eye. They pat him on the back in excitement.

I stop and take a deep breath, inhaling the rich smell of cedar. I could get used to this.

I hear my name being called through the roar of laughter. "Garret, over here!"

At the far end of the hatchet-throwing rows, I see my three friends huddled around a tall wooden table, each of them holding beers in their hands. I immediately notice an extra beer on the tabletop, standing by itself. I hope that's for me.

I make my way through the crowd toward my friends, occasionally having to shove myself between groups of overly-exuberant twenty-somethings. As I get closer, I notice the guys are all still dressed in their slacks and button-up shirts, but their sleeves are rolled up and their top buttons undone.

"Ready to throw some hatchets?" John, the nerdiest of my friends, asks, greeting me first.

"Hey, man. Glad you could make it," Alex, the tallest of my friends, says, coming around the table and giving me a hug.

"Me too. I wasn't sure my flight was going to get back in time. I landed about an hour ago and got here as quickly as I could."

Alex slides the beer towards me. "Not sure what kind you like, so we just guessed."

I grab it and take a sip. It's not my favorite, but I'm grateful. "Thanks, man. This is perfect. This place is pretty crazy. I'm not sure how I feel about throwing hatchets."

"I came here a few weeks ago with another group of friends and we had a blast," says John. "Trust me, it's almost cathartic."

I look around, confused. "Wasn't Damien standing here before? I swear I saw him."

Alex laughs. "You know him. That guy can barely hold his bladder better than a toddler. He decided to hit the bathroom one more time before we got started."

"Ha, yeah. I hate going on sales trips with him. We're always having to stop every thirty minutes."

"So, what have you been up to, man?" John asks. "You're never around anymore."

"Remember I told you about that girl in L.A.? Kora?"

"The singer?" Alex asks.

"Yeah, her. Well, we almost broke up. Actually, we did break up for a few weeks. She found out about Amelia and wanted nothing to do with me anymore."

"Oh," Alex says. "How'd that happen?"

"I don't know. I guess I seemed a little too suspicious. I was staying with her during the week, but I always left every weekend. She kind of guessed it on her own."

"Wow, that sucks, man. Sorry," John says.

I shake my head. "No, trust me. It's fine. I went down to see her yesterday. We made up. I promised her whatever she wanted to hear so we could get back together."

"Like what?" Damien asks as he approaches the table.

"Hey, man," I say, grabbing his hand and throwing my other arm around his shoulders. "Good to see you."

"You too," he says. "Now, what did you tell her? How in the world did you get two women to be okay with each other?"

"Well, Amelia doesn't know about her. She definitely would not be okay, but all I had to do was tell Kora that I'm in the process of leaving Amelia and that eventually, we'll be together."

"And she believed it?" Damien asks, surprised.

I nod and take a large swig of my beer.

"Man, no wonder you're such a good salesman," John comments, chuckling.

"Yeah, she believed it. Who knows? Maybe I will leave Amelia. I do really like this girl," I admit.

Daniel shakes his head. "You're the man. I wouldn't even contemplate doing something like that."

"You know what's really crazy?" I say. "My wedding anniversary is coming up. So, I went and bought Amelia this necklace that I knew she would love. Well, when I was there picking it out, I realized I could get a two-for-one deal with this. So I bought one for Kora, too. I'm planning on giving one to Amelia for our anniversary and gave one to Kora just yesterday."

"Two for one. Wow, dude," Alex says. "You're insane."

I shrug. "They're never gonna meet each other. What's to lose?"

THE MEMORY BEGINS to fade and I realize that I am no longer in the hatchet-throwing bar; instead, I'm in the prison resort banquet hall. Several people are calling my name and walking toward me, led by Pat, the doctor's husband. Great. Why can't they just leave me alone?

Pat stops just a few feet in front of me and crosses his arms. "We've all been talking and it's pretty clear that you are the most suspicious one of us. We don't have time to wait for the authorities to arrive. None of us can afford to get stuck here for days," Pat announces. "So, we're going to do a little investigating ourselves to help move the process along."

I put up my hands. "We've already been over this. I didn't do anything."

"We'll see about that," he says. "If you didn't do anything, you'll answer a few of our questions."

I look around me and notice at least a half-dozen people standing there, effectively backing me into a corner. They are all looking at me angrily.

If I have nothing to hide, I shouldn't be afraid to talk to them. But then again, who's to say they won't twist my words? I do know that if I don't talk, then they'll just make something up and that could be way worse. "Fine," I say. "What do you want to know?"

"You knew Kora, right?" Pat asks.

I hesitate. The last few times they've asked me this question, I've denied it, but it's obvious they don't believe me.

Maybe this truth is something I can give them without making myself look too suspicious. "Yes, I knew her. I met her in L.A. on business."

"And how exactly did you know her? Were you friends? Were you in a relationship?"

Panic rises in me. I can't have any of this getting back to Amelia. What do I tell them? "What does it matter how I knew her?"

"Motives matter," Pat says. "We're trying to ascertain if you had one."

I sigh. "We were friends. That's it."

"Interesting," Pat says skeptically.

The blonde-haired woman looks at me. "Didn't look like you were friends the way she looked at you last night when she was on stage."

"I think we were just both shocked to see each other here. I had no idea she was going to be here," I explain.

Another voice from the back of the crowd pipes up. "You really had no idea she was going to be here?"

"No, I swear. It was a complete shock to me, which is why I left last night at dinner."

"Wouldn't you be happy to see a friend and not feel sick to your stomach about it?" Pat asks, his eyes narrowing.

"It was just a shock," I insist. "That's it. Nothing more. I went to the bathroom and threw up. That's all. And I've been feeling sick ever since. I didn't do anything to Kora."

"Come on, guys." A small brunette woman speaks up to the crowd, "He's not going to tell us anything. This is pointless. Let's just leave him alone. The truth will come to light, it always does."

"Just know we have our eyes on you," Pat warns before walking away.

My adrenaline is racing as they all walk away from me. They think I did this. They think I killed Kora. How can I convince them it's not true? Beads of sweat form on my brow as my heartbeat continues to rise and I begin to panic.

25

AMELIA (PRESENT)

We walk into a room with what appears to be a working generator. Confused, I look at Miles. "What's the problem with this thing?" I ask. "It looks like it's working."

He shakes his head. "Nothing is wrong with it. It's working exactly as it's supposed to. It's not meant to give power to the entire hotel like I told everybody else. I just needed an excuse to get someone in here to help me with something else."

The cook, Sarah, looks at Miles, offended. "So you lied to us?"

"Yes, but I had no choice. Trust me. If you just suspend your frustration with me for just a moment, I'll explain everything," Miles responds.

"Okay," the cook says. "I'm listening."

"At the time of Kora's death, the camera system was on. If it was foul play, I'm pretty sure that there's video footage of the killer coming in or out of her room. The problem is that the video camera system is not one of those things that is supposed to receive power from the generator. It's considered a luxury, not a necessity."

"You told us that you weren't sure if it was foul play," says Sarah.

"Right... well, we are not sure," says Miles. "Honestly, I'm treating this thing as if she was murdered, until we're all safe. I just haven't told the others that I feel that way."

Sarah and I look at each other uneasily.

Miles continues. "We want to be sure though. I don't know why they didn't think the cameras were a necessity yet."

"That makes sense," I say. "Who cares what the cameras catch if people are dying from the cold, right?"

Miles nods. "Exactly."

"So, what are you proposing?" I ask.

"Well, I was hoping you could help me somehow wire some extra power from the generator to the computer that holds all of the video footage."

I look at the generator hesitantly and then back at Miles. "I do have some experience with generators, but it was a long time ago when I was a kid. I'm not sure that I know how to do this."

"Listen, the real reason that you're here is that I trust you. You too," he says, nodding to Sarah. "I don't believe you guys had anything to do with Kora's death. We need to keep this a secret between the three of us so that the killer doesn't find out that there might be footage of the murder."

"How are you so certain that it's not one of us?" I ask suspiciously.

"Well, Sarah was in the middle of prep for dinner. She was actually with me when I found Kora..."

I study Sarah. She takes a breath and nods, confirming his story. Clearly, this has been a hard night for her.

Miles continues. "And Amelia, I saw you several times as you were looking for your MIA husband. You don't need intuition to come to the conclusion that you or Sarah probably didn't do it. I mean, what motive could you possibly have?"

His logic sounds completely ridiculous to me; none of those reasons prove anything.

He continues. "Look, I don't think this is going to be hard. I could probably figure it out by myself. I brought you two because I had to make sure I got people back here that I knew I could trust."

"But we volunteered, you didn't ask us. How did you control that?" I say, increasingly uncertain about this man's people skills.

"I didn't know for sure, but I was hoping you would. Let's just call it a hunch, but I had a feeling you would raise your hand even if you didn't actually know anything about generators."

"What gave me away, my shining personality?" I say, laughing.

"No, but you just kind of seem a little no-nonsense, like the type of person that's willing to get their hands dirty, even if they aren't an expert at something if it's to help someone else."

"Yeah, that pretty much sums me up," I say. "I'm always willing to help."

"I sensed that from you. So I had a feeling you would raise your hand."

"What about me? I volunteered, too."

"Yeah, I didn't expect her to want someone to go with her, but as soon as I saw it was you, I knew it was going to be okay."

"Sounds like you got pretty lucky," I say skeptically.

"You can call it luck if you want, but I read people. I've been doing it for years as part of my job and as a result, I can pretty accurately predict their behavior. It's really a finely honed skill."

I shake my head. That's what someone entirely full of themselves would say. I'm not so sure I trust him as much as he seems to trust me. There's no way I'm letting him get his hands on this generator. "Well, where do we start?" I ask. Hopefully, he doesn't ask to participate.

"Here's a wrench," he says, handing me a large metal wrench. "Do you think you can figure it out yourself? I probably should make sure the rest of the guests are doing okay."

"Don't worry, we got this," I tell him with confidence I'm not actually feeling.

I take my camera off of my shoulder and set it down next to the generator. I would never forgive myself if I somehow ruined it. I start opening panels and inspecting the wires that are already running in and out of the machine.

I look up and see Miles exiting the room. "Hey," I yell.

He turns back around, an expectant look on his face. "Yes?" He asks.

"Do you have any extra auxiliary cords?" I ask.

He walks to the corner of the room and grabs a bunch of cords. He then walks over to me and places them on my lap. "Anything else?"

"I could use some additional tools, just in case."

"Ok, I'll go hunt some down in the storage room. If you need me before I find them, send Sarah to come get me."

"Wait, so we're splitting up?" Sarah asks.

"Only if you trust me," Miles says. "Only if the three of us trust each other."

Sarah eyes the both of us and then shakes off any suspicion. "Yeah, I mean. I guess I just want us to be safe."

I can tell she's just trying to convince herself that he's trustworthy. "It's faster if we split up when we need to. Faster is safer," I say.

"Okay. That makes sense," says Sarah.

Miles nods at her and exits the room. When he disappears down the hall, Sarah turns to me.

"You think you can do it?" Sarah asks.

"No clue, but here goes nothing," I say as I start plugging cords into the generator. "I hope I don't blow this thing up."

26

MILES

I walk down the hallway towards the storage room. When I'm sure that no one is around, I let the grief hit me like a tidal wave, overwhelming me and drowning me in a sea of memories and regret. I can't believe she's gone. It's all my fault. If I hadn't asked her to come here, she wouldn't be dead. I slump to the floor, unable to move. The guilt is so heavy on my heart that it makes my legs physically unable to walk. What have I done? Why did she agree to come here? The memory of the first time I saw her again comes barreling in.

~

I STOOD behind the front desk, arranging all the office supplies in preparation for opening night in a couple of weeks.

"Where do you want me to put this, boss?"

I looked up and found one of the newly hired front desk employees standing in front of me. He was holding a large potted ficus plant and was straining with the weight of it.

"Put it over there," I said, pointing to the corner of the room. "This room could use some life."

"I can't believe they turned this prison into a hotel," he said. "Who's going to actually come here?"

"You'd be surprised," I replied, shaking my head. "We've had a lot of interest, mostly from people who are just plain curious about being inside of a prison. Plus, there are the hipsters who love stuff like this. It's kind of one of those novelty things, like staying in a hotel made of ice. I mean, who would want to sleep on a bed of ice? But people do it."

"You're right," he said. "There are some weird people out there."

I laughed. "There definitely are."

The front door to the main lobby opened and a woman walked in. She was wearing a long fur coat, sunglasses and a white beanie. She took off her glasses and my heart stopped. It had been years since I had last seen her, but the effect she had on me was the same as it was when I first saw her in college. My limbs were weak and I could barely catch my breath. She was still the most beautiful woman I had ever seen.

I stepped out from behind the desk and walked towards her. "Kora, I'm so glad you could make it."

"Miles, it's been forever," she said. "This place is. . . interesting."

"I know, right? Nothing like feeling like you're going away for twenty years to life when you're on vacation."

She laughed. "I'm not sure I would stay here for fun, but people do some crazy things."

"You have no idea the things that I've seen in this business." I gave her a brief hug and then stepped back. "You look good."

"Thanks, so do you. So tell me, what are your plans? How can I help?" She asked.

"Well, we have a soft opening in a couple of weeks. A select number of couples will be coming to test out the amenities. We gave them a deep discount because we know there'll be a lot of kinks, but we still want to treat them well. So, we're going to have an elegant dinner for them the first night and we need some entertainment."

"And you want me to be the entertainment?" She questioned.

I grabbed her hand. "Kora, I know it's been a long time since I've seen you, but I have always believed you deserve to be famous. Your voice is that good. I not only want you to sing for this soft opening, but I would also love you to be our entertainment every weekend."

She put her hand on her chest. "Wow, that is quite the honor, but I'm not sure I can afford to give up all my gigs on the weekends."

"This could be a big break for you. We already have a lot of interest from some very high-profile people. All it takes is one of them to believe in you and your career could skyrocket."

She was quiet for several seconds and then she sighed. "You just invited me here and didn't tell me why. What are you going to do if I say no?"

I smiled at her sheepishly.

She shook her head. "I can't commit to every weekend, but I'm willing to give it a try. I'll do the first weekend for you."

"Excellent," I said, clapping my hands. "Trust me, I will compensate you well."

She held out both her hands, seemingly to quell my excitement. "I'm not doing this for the money, Miles. I'm doing this for you. I want you to be successful. We had our good days back then, didn't we?"

"The best," I replied. "Remember that trip we made to the Carlsbad Caverns?"

"Remember it? I think it scarred me for life."

A smile formed on my lips. "You were terrified when they told us we had to descend down that rope to get into the cave, but you did it," I said. "I was so proud of you."

"Yeah, that was one of the hardest things I've ever done, but I honestly couldn't have done it without you by my side. I'll never forget those moments."

I stared at her and a pang of sadness ripped through me. I was a fool to let her go, but now here she stood, right in front of me and because of my position here at the resort, I had to make sure that no one knew we had any kind of history. I took a deep breath. "I do have one request," I said. "I don't think that people should know that we were together or that we even know each other."

She looked at me suspiciously. "What's the need to lie, Miles? Who cares what we once were to each other and that we're friends?"

I panicked. I hadn't expected that kind of reaction from her. "I know it sounds weird, but I just don't want the guests to feel like there's something going on between us. This has to be strictly professional."

"Are you saying I can't be professional and still be your friend?"

"No, I'm not trying to say that." Man, this was getting out of control and I hadn't planned on her being so defensive. "Listen, Kora. Why does anybody need to know that we used to know each other? As far as they're concerned, none of that matters."

She crossed her arms. "Glad to know that none of it mattered to you."

"Just stop. That's not what I'm saying."

"Then what are you trying to say?" She asked.

"Honestly, it's not really about the guests or you being professional. I mostly just don't want the rest of the staff to know that you and I have a history," I explained. "I don't want them feeling like I'm giving you special privileges or paying you more or something like that because you're my friend. I need them on their game during opening weekend. There can't be a hint of jealousy going on if we're going to pull this off."

She stared at me suspiciously. "Why didn't you say that from the beginning? Of course, I don't want the rest of the staff to be jealous of me. I'll pretend I don't know you."

I sighed, grateful that she was finally on board. "Shall I show you to the stage?"

She nodded and as we walked toward the stage, I couldn't help but feel regret. Why had I ever let her go? We were so good together. I had never loved anyone like I loved her.

SITTING on the cold prison floor, I am devastated by all I have lost. I had hoped that this would be our second chance. I thought that maybe I could figure out a way to remind her of the love we once had for each other and she would take me back. But now, sitting in the silence of these empty halls, I am utterly aware that my hopes are never going to be realized. Kora's gone and I'm left here alone.

27

GARRET

I stare at the group of people who were just interrogating me; they are huddled together, talking in hushed whispers. Occasionally, one or two of them glance in my direction. It's obvious they're talking about me. I shake my head. How did I end up the suspect in this? Here I am, grieving the loss of the woman I love and everybody only wants to point their fingers at me and accuse me of killing her.

So much has changed in the last twelve hours. I think back to last night when I first saw Kora at dinner, initially I was mortified. I didn't understand how Amelia and I ended up at the same resort as Kora. It seemed like too much of a coincidence.

I'll never forget the look on Amelia's face when she realized that Kora had the exact same necklace as her. I've never felt more stupid in my life. Here I was, arrogant enough to believe that they would never meet each other, so it was no big deal. Then they were face to face and it was glaringly obvious to Amelia that there was something between me and Kora. I've been contemplating telling Amelia for a while, but it wasn't supposed to happen like this.

I glance around the room. I know Miles said not to go anywhere by ourselves, but I can't be here anymore. The weight of my grief is almost more than I can bear; I can't keep allowing them to add to it with their stares and accusations. I feel trapped and panic begins to rise in my chest. Beads of sweat form on my brow and I wipe them off with my bare hand. My breath comes in short, ragged gasps.

I stand and look around the room for the quickest and most discrete way out. In the far back corner, far away from the couches that the couples have been using as make-shift beds, there is an exit door. I glance over at the crowd. Many of them have decided to lie down in an attempt to get some sleep. Those that are still awake are huddled in small groups. For the time being, I'm not being watched. I think I could slip out of here without anyone noticing.

I creep towards the back door, putting gentle pressure on it, praying it doesn't creak when I open it. The door handle clicks quietly as I turn it, sweat dripping down my forehead. My vision is becoming blurred as the panic rises even further. I slowly push the door open and it's silent, this provides a modicum of relief and I can sense the panic dissipating slightly.

I squeeze my way through the entrance into the dark hallway, closing the door quietly behind me. The lights are not on in here. I can barely see two feet in front of my face. I reach into my pocket and grab my phone. I've been trying to save the battery, but this is an emergency. If I don't get away from these people, I might explode.

I turn on the phone and groan. There's only twenty percent battery remaining. I have to be strategic about how I use this thing. Right now, I need light. I turn on the flashlight and shine it down the hall.

The hallway stretches before me like a dark, forgotten passage, its length shrouded in shadows. There isn't the faintest hint of light. I shudder at the thought of walking down this hallway toward the darkness.

It feels as though I'm in a horror movie, the ones where I'm always yelling at the screen, telling the character to turn around. They never do and I'm always frustrated that they would make such a stupid decision, but now I think I get it. Sometimes, the darkness in front of you feels safer than what's behind you. I choose the unknown. At least in the darkness, I can hide.

28

GARRET

I open the door to the large block where our hotel room is. The room is silent and ominous. There are no lights on, plunging everything into pitch blackness. If I believed in ghosts, I would be terrified. Heck, I'm pretty terrified even without believing in ghosts, to be honest.

I slowly make my way up the steps towards our room. As soon as I reach the room and pull open the heavy door, I'm met with a space even darker than the large room, if that's even possible. The flashlight on my phone barely illuminates the darkness. I head straight towards the liquor cart and pour myself a glass of bourbon. I take a long, deep sip and relish the burning sensation down my throat. It seems to help dim the fire burning inside me.

The darkness of this hotel room is suffocating. The walls feel like they're closing in on me and I begin to pace back and forth. I can't stay here any longer. Nobody, including my own wife, believes me. The suspicious gazes of the other hotel guests feel like they are drilling into me.

If that was all it was, I could handle it, but I know they're also not done asking me questions. They're going to pick and pry until I give in and tell them everything, ruining myself in the process. I can't stay here. I can't put myself at that kind of risk.

I grab a suitcase and pack everything I'm going to need, making sure the essentials are all in this bag, including a few changes of underwear and socks, along with every warm piece of clothing that I own. As I pack my stuff, my mind races with thoughts of Kora. I can't believe she's dead. I loved her so much.

Seeing her yesterday while sitting next to Amelia was mind-opening for me. I looked at Kora and looked at Amelia and I realized that I had nothing left for Amelia. All of my love and everything belonged to Kora. The moment I saw Kora yesterday, I knew I had messed up.

Why couldn't she have just been patient with me? What if patience was all it took to save us? She had given me a second chance to make things work between us, but a couple of months ago, she just completely cut me off without warning. Yesterday was the first time I had seen her in a long time.

If she really loved me, she would have just waited and none of this would have happened. The one real person that I cared for in this world, no longer exists. I should have left Amelia months ago to be with her and now it's too late.

I want to go to her and hug her one last time, but I can't. If someone were to see me going into her room, that would only make me look more guilty than I already do. I can't afford to be implicated in her murder. My freedom feels like the only thing I have left and I have to protect it at all costs.

"I'm so sorry, Kora," I sob. "I wish things could have been different, but now that you're gone, I have to save myself."

I grab my bag and carry it down the stairs to the door that leads outside. I open it up and am taken aback by the burst of cold wind. It bites my face and stings my throat. I gasp. I don't know if I can do this, but then I think about the mob back in the banquet hall and I realize I have no choice. They're going to crucify me without a trial if I stay here. They've already deemed me guilty. Who knows what else they'll do?

I think I saw a village just a couple of miles from here on our way up the mountain. I can walk two miles, even in a blizzard, if that's what it takes to get away from the mob. I take a step into the snow and brace myself against the cold. I cover my entire face with a scarf, except for my eyes and begin to trudge slowly, but surely, through the snow towards the road that leads to safety.

29

GARRET

The trek from the outside door to the front of the resort takes me nearly thirty minutes. I glance at my phone; there's only fifteen percent battery left. I turn it off to conserve power. I have to make sure I have a way to call for help if I get lost or stuck.

I continue forward, setting off down what I think is the main road to town. It's not as dark outside as it was in the hotel room, but it's still dark and I am having a difficult time seeing. It doesn't help that the snow has picked up and is swirling around me, clouding my vision and biting the little bits of skin I still have exposed around my eyes. Snowflakes land on my eyelashes and congregate there until they are melted by the heat of my body.

After what feels like hours of trudging through deep snow, I stop and look around me. I can't even tell where the trees start and the road ends. Does the road continue in front of me? Or is that a forest? I reach into my pocket and pull out the jade pendant and necklace. I let it drop into the deep snow. It instantly disappears and I breathe a sigh of relief. Very quickly, I realize that I don't know where I am; it dawns on me that I've been completely foolish.

There's no way I'm going to get to the town alive in this mess. I never should have left the resort. What was I thinking? At least back at the resort, my enemies were only hell-bent on destroying my life, not taking it away from me entirely. At least, I hope, but then again, there's already one dead body. Who's to say that I'm not next?

I stand for several minutes, contemplating my safest option. Do I continue towards the town and potentially die of frostbite and hypothermia? Or do I make my way back to the resort only to be attacked once again by the committee of vultures? It's a no-brainer, really. Dying of hypothermia is not on my agenda for today. At least at the resort, I can hide somewhere and hopefully never be found.

I turn around, hoping that if I move forward, I'll be able to find my way back to the resort. Even if I don't, I know that in order to stay alive, I have to keep moving and generating body heat. If I don't, I'll be dead in minutes.

I focus on putting one foot in front of the other. The sound of my steps crunching in the snow is rhythmic and almost soothing. The storm swirls endlessly around me, nearly blinding me. The cold bites at my skin and the wind howls in my ears. Each breath I take is a struggle as it feels like I'm breathing in a thousand tiny needles. I want desperately to stop, maybe find shelter in the trees, but I know I have to keep moving if I want to survive.

After several minutes of walking in the direction I believed the resort was in, I start to wonder if I'll ever find it. I should have reached it by now if I was heading in the right direction, but it seems as far away now as it did when I started. I haven't run into any trees yet, so I'm hopeful I'm still on the road.

I stumble and stagger as my body grows more and more weary. I begin to wonder if I'm just walking in circles. Just keep moving. Just keep moving. Movement is the only hope that I have of finding shelter, whether it's in the village or in the resort; I no longer care. I know for sure if I'm out here much longer, I'm going to die.

30

GARRET (PAST)

I stare out the small window as the plane begins its descent. The Vegas lights are bright as we approach. I've spent almost the entire flight thinking about Kora. I want to make this work between us, but I'm not quite sure how. Actually leaving Amelia is the least of my worries. The thought of my parents disowning me because I signed a bad prenup devastates me. I have to figure something else out.

Suddenly, the plane drops several feet as we hit a pocket of air. I grasp the armrests, my knuckles turning white. I hate this part. Most of the time when I'm flying, I can convince myself that we're just traveling really quickly on the ground, especially when the plane moves smoothly through the air, but when we hit turbulence and drop like this, the realization that I'm thousands of feet above the ground in a giant metal flying bucket becomes all too real.

I grab the mini vodka I'd purchased from the flight attendant earlier, unscrew the cap and down it quickly. I take a deep breath. The person next to me is sleeping soundly through the whole thing. I shake my head. I have no idea how people do that. The plane continues to bump and jolt until we finally land on the ground fifteen minutes later. My shirt is drenched in sweat and I've had to wipe my face off with a napkin several times.

As we taxi to the gate, the adrenaline coursing through me begins to dissipate, leaving me feeling exhausted. Not having to fly so often would be another amazing benefit of Kora moving here. I'll still have business in L.A., but I should be able to manage that in one week a month. There's no reason for me to be there every week. I only do it now because of Kora.

I grab my bags and a rideshare picks me up just outside of baggage claim. The landscape flashes by, a neon oasis in the desert night.

I check my phone and see a text message from Amelia. *I have a surprise for you when you get home.* My heart sinks. Great, what kind of surprise could she have for me? These situations never end well. Either she gets sad because I don't react the way she wants me to, or she gets angry because I don't have something to give her in return.

It's a lose-lose situation for me. I could give her the jade necklace, the one that's a duplicate of Kora's, but then what would I have for our anniversary weekend? Shaking my head, I decide I'm better off dealing with the consequences and saving the necklace for our anniversary.

The rideshare pulls to a stop in front of the house and I slowly get out. I grab my bags from the trunk, close the door and walk towards the front of the house. As soon as I'm on the property, the motion sensor light turns on, alerting Amelia to my arrival. My stomach drops as she opens the door. She's standing in the door frame in a lacy negligee and I can't help but feel a pang of guilt and regret for straying so far away.

"Surprise," she says seductively.

Standing in front of me is a hint of the woman I used to know, but instead of turning me on, it just makes me both sad and annoyed at the same time. How did things go so far astray? While my feelings for her were never the same as my feelings for Kora, I did love her once and now I dread even having to be around her. It's not supposed to be like this.

"What is all this?" I ask, hoping to buy myself some time.

"I just made you a little something, thought we could have a romantic evening together."

I loosen my tie and unbutton the top button. "I don't know Amelia. I'm tired. It's been a long week."

Disappointment crosses her face and my guilt slaps me upside the head. She's my wife. I should want this. "Okay, fine. Just give me a few minutes to freshen up."

A smile bursts across her face, almost as if just saying yes was gift enough.

Twenty minutes later, I come down the stairs in my sweats and sweatshirt. It's not as fancy as her negligee, but if I'm going to do this, I need to be comfortable.

She's sitting at the dinner table with prime rib, asparagus and mashed potatoes expertly plated in front of her.

"Babe, did you make that?" I ask, surprised.

She nods. "I know I'm not the greatest cook, but this seems to have turned out okay."

I nod enthusiastically. "It looks amazing." I pull out my chair and sit down, taking in the aroma of charred meat and spices.

"Let me cut you a piece," she says, standing from the table. She grabs a long knife and slices a thin piece of prime rib, then lays it on my plate. She then scoops some mashed potatoes and grabs a handful of asparagus, setting them down next to the pink piece of meat.

"Wow, Amelia, thank you so much," I say, genuinely appreciating the surprise. My earlier hesitation somewhat diminishes as the dinner progresses. Our conversation flows easily, reminiscent of how we used to be in the earlier days of our marriage. I'm reminded of how much I used to care about this woman. Yet, despite the smooth conversation, my feelings remain unchanged; I'm still in love with Kora.

Dinner finishes. Amelia stands from the table and forms a seductive pose with one hand on the counter and another on her hip. I inwardly groan. There's no escaping it. I'm going to have to be intimate with her. I haven't been physically attracted to her in years. Even now, as she stands in front of me, barely clothed, I find myself feeling nothing.

I walk towards her and put my hands on her face. Maybe kissing her will help me change how I feel. I lean down and give her a deep kiss. It definitely helps, but I'm still not quite ready to sleep with her.

She grabs my hand and leads me towards the stairs.

Reluctantly, I follow her as she heads to our bedroom. As we walk, I picture Kora — the curves of her body, the smoothness of her skin. I know it's wrong, but I have to do something to prepare myself for the night with my wife. I'm aware I sound like an awful person, but I have no other choice. I'm not ready for Amelia to find out about Kora. Not yet. I have plans to make and set in motion before that can happen, but it is obvious to me that my marriage is all but over.

31

MILES (PRESENT)

I'm supposed to be getting supplies, but that was really just an excuse to leave the room. I couldn't let Amelia and Sarah see me cry and the tears have been slowly building behind my eyes all night. I had to leave before I lost control and could no longer hold them back. I knew that once I let go, they were going to stream down my face, an unstoppable flood of grief and regret.

The weight of everything I've lost tonight bears down heavily on my shoulders. Kora was the love of my life and I had high hopes that by spending more time with me here at the resort, she would fall back in love with me. I never stopped loving her. No matter how many dates I went on over the years, I always compared them to Kora and they never measured up.

I had a few relationships, most of them lasting only a few months. In each one, I hoped that maybe, as time wore on, my feelings would change, but they never did. Whoever I was with was never Kora and I ended up breaking things off and walking away.

When Kora agreed to take this gig, I felt like it was my

chance to win her back. I knew it was a long shot, but I was determined to seize the opportunity with everything that was in me, but now, she's dead and my hopes of ever finding love and getting married died with her.

Now, every woman I meet has even less of a chance of winning my heart because not only do they have to compete with who she was, but they also have to compete with my inflated memory of her. I know it's unfair, but I can't help it. I'm probably going to be alone for the rest of my life.

I walk down the hall towards Kora's room, needing to see her just one more time before the police arrive and take her away. I open the door quietly, trying not to make a sound. I know that everyone is in the banquet hall, yet I still feel the need to be cautious. No one's supposed to be in this room so that we can preserve the evidence of her killer, but I'm the one who found her. Going in here one more time can't do additional harm, can it?

I step into the room. It's pitch black. My heart pounds heavily in my chest. Somewhere on the floor in front of me is the dead body of the woman I love. Maybe this was all a horrible nightmare and she's not there anymore. Maybe I dreamed this whole thing up and I still have a chance at love.

I turn the light on my phone and shine it on the floor, where I remember finding her body. She's still there. The small irrational hope I had been clinging to dies in that second. This is not a dream.

I take a closer look at her body. There's no blood on her. I have no idea what killed her, even though the doctor believes it was foul play. I couldn't tell everyone the full story. I don't believe it myself.

Kora's curly hair spills out around her face and she

almost looks like she's sleeping peacefully on the floor, but her still, lifeless body tells the truth.

"Kora, why?" I whisper through my tears as the dam finally breaks open. I sink to the ground, my back against the wall, my body wracked with sobs. I cry until there are no more tears left. I feel beaten down and hopeless. This wasn't supposed to end like this.

After several minutes, I take a deep breath. I have to hold it together. Nobody can know about my relationship with Kora. They must all believe she was just my employee, or I too, will become a suspect in her death.

I wipe my face and stand, shining the light around the room. I walk over to a bulletin board on the wall. It's covered in pictures. I study each one. Most of them are of people and places she experienced either before or after me.

My heart stops as I come across a picture I recognize. It was taken in Kora's dorm room back when we were in college. In the photo, we are sitting on the bed together. Kora sits in front of me, her head leaning back against my chest. My arms are wrapped around her waist.

In the picture, she's smiling towards the camera, a genuine look of happiness on her face. I however, am not looking at the camera. Instead, I'm looking at her, a look of adoration on my face. I can't believe she kept this. Maybe she still had feelings for me. That thought intensifies my grief. I put my hand on the wall to brace myself and take deep breaths to control my emotions.

As I'm leaning against the wall, it hits me: this picture is evidence that we knew each other. It wouldn't be too hard for a detective to put two and two together and then I become one of their prime suspects. I can't let that happen. This can't be here when the authorities come. I quickly pull the pushpin out of the corkboard and remove the picture, slipping it into my back pocket. As I'm replacing the push-pin, I hear a noise in the hallway.

Crap. I should have closed the door. I quickly turn off the phone flashlight and make my way in the dark to a corner of the room that can't be seen from the hallway. I stand in the corner as still as possible. A flashlight beam bounces around the hallway outside the door. The person carrying the light briefly shines it into the room, sweeping the light around. The light pauses for a moment on Kora's lifeless body before continuing its path around the room.

My heart stops. What if they see me? What if someone knows I'm in here, tampering with evidence? The light moves on, never reaching me.

Who is that holding the light? I can't quite tell. The person backs out of the room and continues down the hallway. For a split second, the light bouncing off the walls in the corridor illuminates their face. Is that Amelia?

What is she doing here? Isn't she fixing the generator? Confusion floods through me as I hear her footsteps diminish as she approaches the end of the corridor. What is that woman up to?

32

AMELIA

I slowly open the door to the generator room and see Sarah sitting on the other side, leaning against the wall. She rubs her eyes and then stretches her arms up to the sky as if she was just waking up.

"Did you fall asleep?" I say smirking.

"That took you way longer than you said it would. What did you expect?" She shrugs.

"Yeah, you wouldn't believe how hard it is to find the bathroom in the pitch black. Even with a flashlight, I could barely see a few feet in front of my face. I wasn't quite sure where I was going," I reply.

"Was it creepy walking around a prison in the dark?" She asks.

"I tried not to think about it, but yeah. Every time I allowed myself to contemplate where I was, I got a little creeped out. Especially when I found myself in the wing where our rooms are. I shined the light on those prison bars and nearly peed myself."

"Um, yeah, that's why I'm trying to hold it as long as I

can, at least until morning. I'm not going to the bathroom at night unless I have no other choice," she says.

I chuckle. "Probably smart."

I get back to work on the generator. I've been able to attach the extension cord to the generator itself, but now I need to get it to the computer. "Can you hold the flashlight for me and shine it under the table?" I ask Sarah.

"Sure. Finally, something to do," she says enthusiastically.

I crawl under the computer desk, looking for the plug. There are dozens of cords underneath, each going in a different direction. The light of the flashlight on the cords casts eery shadows on the wall.

"Why are there so many of these?" I mutter. "I have no idea which one is which." I raise my hand to the back of the computer, hunting around for the power cord. Finally, I find it towards the edge of the box. I grab the cord and follow it down, eventually discovering the other end. "Got it," I say out loud.

I grab the extension cord and the end of the power cord and connect them. At first, nothing happens. I crawl back out from underneath the desk and stand in front of the machine, perplexed.

"I'm pretty sure I connected the cord correctly to the generator. Why isn't it working?"

"Um, I'm not an expert," Sarah says. "But maybe you just need to turn it on?"

I slap my hand against my forehead. How could I be so dense? "I was just testing you," I tease.

"Right, we'll go with that," she says, smiling.

A brief jolt of anxiety hits me out of nowhere as I glance toward her. I was expecting a friendly smile on her face, but instead, her smile looks eerie in the glow of the flashlight.

Almost diabolical. I quickly turn away toward the monitor. It's just the light. She's not trying to kill me, right? I shrug off the feeling and focus on the computer.

I press the power button on the machine itself and then turn on the monitor. At first, the only evidence that there's power to the computer is a little green light glowing from the power button, but after a few seconds, it begins to boot up.

"You did it," Sarah exclaims.

"We did it," I respond.

"I was just here for moral support and to hold the flashlight."

"Well, you were very supportive," I say with a grin.

Thanks," she says, chuckling.

We both resume our positions on the floor up against the wall. "You'll never believe what I saw in the hallway."

"Really? What?" She asks.

"When I was trying to find the bathroom, most of the doors were closed, but there was one door that was open. I shined my light in the room out of curiosity and saw nothing at first, but then I shined the light on the floor and there, in the middle of the room, was the body of Kora," I say in a hushed whisper.

She gasps. "She's still just lying there in the open?"

I nod. "I thought you knew."

"I left when the doctor started checking everything out. I was pretty freaked out. It's all so crazy."

"I know, right? But yeah the door was wide open. Why would they leave it like that?"

Sarah shrugs. "I have no idea. Wouldn't that make it so the crime scene could be contaminated?"

"That's what I was thinking. I actually heard some noises when I was walking down the hall and I thought someone was in the room. That's why I looked inside to begin with. I shined the light all about the room, but I didn't see anyone other than Kora. They could have been hiding in the corners, but I wasn't about to go all the way into a room with a dead body."

"Yeah, you wouldn't catch me willingly hanging in a room with a dead body either," Sarah agrees. "It's just so weird."

"Right, completely weird."

"Did you close the door?" She asks.

"No, I didn't want anyone knowing that I went down there and saw it. I left it exactly as I found it."

"That makes sense," she says. "Well, I won't tell anyone you saw it."

"Thanks, Sarah. I didn't think you would."

I glance over at the computer; it's still processing and spinning. Who knows how long it's going to take? These are old computers though, so it's probably going to be a while. "I guess we don't have to wait here for that thing to boot back up. We now know it's working. You ready to head back?"

"Yeah, I need to sleep."

"Me too."

As we walk out of the room, I glance back at the computer. Part of me wants to stay out of curiosity and look at the files myself, but being away from the group for so long doesn't seem smart. What kind of footage is on that thing? Did the security system really capture Kora's true killer?

33

GARRET

I feel like I've been out here for hours, maybe even days. At this point, I've lost all sense of reality. I don't know if I've made any progress during that time. Honestly, I've probably just been wandering in circles. There's no more warmth emanating from my body and I know that my temperature is dangerously close to hypothermic levels.

My brain is in a fog and I can barely think straight. My fingers and toes are numb; I can't wiggle them anymore. If I don't find shelter soon, I'm as good as dead. I have to keep pushing forward. Movement is my only hope. If I stop for even a second, it's over.

I walk for several more minutes through the blizzard. I've always prided myself on being strong and tough, but in this moment, I feel scared, alone and incredibly stupid. How did I let myself get into this predicament? I was so driven by my emotions and a desire not to be the main suspect in Kora's death that I allowed myself to make a completely illogical decision. If I had taken just one minute to think logically through this plan, I would not be in this mess.

The battery on my cell phone is nearly completely dead, the bar says only six percent is left. I know from experience, that means I only have a few minutes left before it shuts off. I shine the light in front of me and it bounces off of the falling snowflakes.

Suddenly, a pair of eyes catches the light. They're like two small, glowing orbs suspended in the darkness. As the light settles on them, they shimmer with a bright, almost otherworldly luminescence.

My heart pounds in my chest. What is that? The part of my mind that is delirious conjures up images of aliens and monsters from the movies I've seen. Fear grips me as I contemplate the end of my life at the hands of this unknown creature. Its eyes stare at me, glowing like twin beacons in the swirling light of the storm. I must be hallucinating. This can't be real, can it?

Its eyes dart away and for a split second, I see the outline of its body. Initially, it looks like a deer, but in my heightened state of anxiety, the figure slowly morphs into something more sinister. Its shape seems to shift and warp in the trembling light, the falling snow adding to its otherworldliness.

I tighten my grip on the flashlight. I thought I might die out here from the cold. I never imagined it would be at the hands of an alien creature. The rational side of my mind tries desperately to talk some sense into my addled, frozen brain. This isn't real. I'm hallucinating from hypothermia and dehydration. If I just close my eyes, it will all go away.

I try to will my eyelids to close, while the other side of my brain screams to keep them open. You have to be able to see to protect yourself. I ignore the thoughts and shut them tightly, all the while praying that I'm right and this is a hallucination.

"This is not real. There is no alien. You're just imagining things," I say out loud.

My voice startles the figure and as I open my eyes, I watch as a deer turns and vanishes into the darkness.

Relief floods my body and I close my eyes once again in resignation. This is it. I'm probably going to die out here. If not from the hypothermia, then from doing something stupid because of a hallucination.

I stand in one place for several moments, recentering myself for one last push for safety. When I open my eyes, I see a tiny prick of light breaking through the storm in the distance. My eyes must be playing tricks on me again. I've been out here for hours and haven't seen a single light.

I close my eyes again and rub them. When I open them, I see it again. A hallucination wouldn't still be there, would it? Maybe it's real. Hope wells up inside me. Maybe I found somebody's house, or maybe it's just a car, but whatever it is, it's all I've got. I put my head down and trudge towards the light. My footsteps become slower and slower with each step. I can feel my body shutting down.

The light grows larger the closer I get to it, but it's not until I'm about ten feet away that I can see it's the resort. Relief floods my body. I made it back. I didn't die in the blizzard.

I walk to the front entrance and open the door. The lights in the lobby are half-dimmed, but they're on. This must be one of the essential rooms. I stumble in, closing the door behind me. The moment I'm in safety, my body begins to shut down.

"Help," I cry, but there's no response. I stumble towards the front desk. Maybe there's somebody sitting behind it. I drop to my hands and knees, my legs no longer able to support my weight. I crawl the rest of the way across the lobby. The unforgiving floor is hard and cold. Each movement sends waves of pain through my throbbing hands and feet, but desperation propels me forward. I call out again. "Help," my voice barely louder than a whisper. Still no answer.

Eventually, I make it to the front desk. I reach up and grab the edge of the counter. I use all the strength I have left to slowly pull myself to a standing position. My knees wobble and my legs shake, barely able to support my weight. My eyes peek over the top of the desk and then widen in shock as they lock with a pair of onyx eyes. All the warmth that was left in my body drains and my legs threaten to give way once more. I'm a dead man.

34

GARRET

Staring at me from behind the desk, wearing headphones and guzzling a bottle of whiskey, sits the man who brought our suitcases up to our room yesterday afternoon. I glance at the name tag prominently pinned on his chest. His name is Bruce. I look back up at him and notice that his eyes haven't left my face. They are fixed on me with an intensity that raises a chill along my spine. The expression on his face is unreadable, his features strong and unmovable like a stone statue. I think he might want to kill me.

I think back to how I treated him when we first got here yesterday. I was rude and demanding when he couldn't find my bag. I basically accused him of being incompetent. What was it he said to me? Something about people going missing or getting lost. Realization dawns on me — he must have been the one who shut the door behind me when I got trapped in that room. It's the only thing that makes sense. I was an asshole to him and he made sure I was punished for it.

This man hates me, I know it, but he's the only one here

and I need his help. I can feel my body slowly getting weaker. My eyelids start to grow heavy as if there are weights fastened to them. I fight to keep them open knowing that as soon as they close, I won't be able to open them back up again. The effort to keep them open is getting harder and harder; I don't have much time left before they shut permanently.

This is my last hope. I take a deep breath and summon the courage to ask for help one last time. "Please, help me. I got lost in the storm and I..." The glare on his face sends shivers down my spine, making the already cold blood in my veins start to freeze and I slip helplessly to the floor from fear and complete exhaustion. My eyelids are impossibly heavy and begin to close. No. I can't go to sleep; he's gonna hurt me. I summon all the energy I have left to force them open, but it's no use. I plunge into darkness.

A FEW SECONDS LATER, I'm conscious again. My eyes flutter open to see the man towering over me. I raise my arms to my head to protect myself from the impending blow. "Please. Don't hurt me," I plead. Bruce leans down towards me. This is it. This is the moment that I die. I try to move my arms to fight back, but it's no use. I barely move them a few inches from my face before they start to fall. "I'm sorry, please..." but I can't even finish my sentence before I'm plunged into darkness once more.

35

AMELIA

Sarah and I walk back into the banquet hall. The earlier commotion has simmered down to a low hum. Several guests and staff are asleep on couches, while others sit at tables, talking in hushed whispers. I search the faces for Garret, but see no sign of him.

Anger surges through me. Did he really leave the banquet hall after being told to stay put? Who does he think he is? It's obvious that Garret only does what he wants without a care for anyone else. The best thing for him to do was to stay here and prove to these people that he was innocent, but no, he had to leave, making himself look guilty all over again. If he looks guilty, then I'm going to look like some kind of accomplice. I have to find him.

I turn to Sarah. "Thanks for your help on the generator," I say, giving her a quick hug. "I couldn't have done it without you."

"No problem," she replies. "I'm a master at holding a flashlight."

I chuckle. "Yes, you are." Her eyes are puffy from exhaustion. "You should get some sleep."

She nods, rubbing her eyes. "I think that's a good idea." She wanders over to an empty couch and lies down.

I turn towards the tables. There are three groups, each with four or five people talking in hushed whispers. I avoid the group with Pat and the Doctor, I already know how they feel about Garret. I'm pretty sure they're not going to be inclined to help me find him.

I turn towards a group on the far side of the dining area. I don't recognize any of the people sitting at the table. Maybe they'll be on my side. I take a deep breath and approach them. The conversation stops as soon as I arrive. I wonder what they were talking about. Was it me or Garret? They all turn and stare at me.

"Hi," I say, wringing my hands. None of them responds. Instead, they just stare at me as if they don't understand the words coming out of my mouth. I continue hesitantly. "Have any of you seen my husband?"

A man with glasses and messy brown hair gives me a wry grin. "We were just talking about that, actually," he says. "He disappeared a while ago. No one knows where he went."

My heart sinks. How could Garret be so stupid? All he had to do was stay here, but no, he couldn't do the one thing that might have saved him.

"It's kind of convenient that he took off after we were all accusing him of murdering that girl," the man adds.

"I'm sure he'll be back," I stammer, although deep down, I'm not sure he will. I don't know this man anymore and I sure as heck can't trust him to do the right thing. He's been living a double life for who knows how long.

I think back to all those weeks he spent away in Los Angeles, leaving me all alone. I could barely get him on the phone during the times he was gone and when I did, he was always curt and unkind, as if I was bothering him. Now I know why.

My heart breaks. Garret has been choosing another woman over me for months now. I wonder how much longer it would have been before he left permanently to start a new life with Kora. He would have left for what? Something new and fresh? Everything gets old over time.

A woman at the table asks, "Do you need anything else?" Her words clearly dismiss me from their presence.

"No, I think I'm just gonna go find him," I reply.

She nods, a stern expression on her face, her disapproval evident. Do these people blame me, too? As if I have any control over Garret's actions.

I walk to the door and open it, stepping foot into the dark hallway. I turn on my flashlight and make my way by memory to the front lobby. If I'm going to find him in this maze of a compound, I need to do it systematically. I'll start from the front and then investigate each corridor one at a time, being careful not to miss anything. If Garret is still in this building, I will find him.

I open the door to the lobby and freeze. The large man who dealt with our bags yesterday is bending over a slumped figure. He wraps his arms around the body and tosses it over his shoulder as if it's a sack of flour. Fear grips me. Is that another dead body? What happened to them?

I hold my breath and inch closer. The figure is wearing Garret's jacket and pants. My stomach drops. Has he been injured? What the hell is going on?

I rush towards the man. "What's happened to him?" I ask. "Is he okay?"

The man just stares at me and continues to walk. "Please stop," I plead. "Let me help him." But my words have no impact. The man continues forward on his path toward the other side of the room. I notice he's walking towards a closed door. What's in that room? Where is he taking him?

"Garret," I yell. "Wake up, Garret. I'm here! I'm here!" I walk behind the man, trying to grab Garret's arm, but it slips from my grasp. It feels cold and lifeless. How is this happening? Is he dead, too?

I watch helplessly as the man unlocks the door and walks into it with Garret. I try to follow behind him, but he shuts the door in my face before I even step one foot into the room. I try to turn the handle, but it's locked. I then raise my fists and pound on the door. "Let me in, that's my husband. Let me in." I pound and yell over and over again, but my cries fall silent in the empty room. That man has my husband and from the looks of it, he might be dead. I eventually give up and drop to the floor.

Garret, what happened to you? I lament. We never should have come here. We should have just had our normal anniversary dinner at the Mexican restaurant. Why did I think that going on a weekend trip to a resort in the middle of nowhere would save my marriage? My marriage has been over for months. This was a terrible idea. Now there's no chance of fixing it if he's dead.

Tears well in my eyes and pour over onto my cheeks. My body is wracked with sobs. How am I going to tell his parents? They already hate me. I stand and slowly make my way back to the banquet hall, tears still streaming down my face. I feel lost and uncertain about what to do next. All I know is I have to tell the rest of the people that none of us are safe.

36

AMELIA

I open the door to the banquet hall, not even attempting to be quiet. All of the people sitting at the table stop talking and turn towards me. Even a few people lying on the couches sit up and stare. I can feel the weight of their eyes on me as I rush in, my chest heaving from the panic that drives my every step. "I found Garret," I blurt out, my voice trembling. "The maintenance man attacked him. I saw it with my own eyes."

A loud buzz erupts around the room and several people stand and walk towards me.

Pat is the first one to speak. "Are you sure?" He asks.

I nod, with tears still glistening on my cheeks. "I went to go find him. I walked into the lobby and saw the man standing over him as if he'd just knocked him down. He then picked him up and carried him away. Garret was unconscious... or worse." I can't bring myself to say the words out loud.

Sarah rushes towards me and puts her arms around me. I hug her back, grateful for her comfort, but after a brief few seconds, I pull away. "I think we're all in danger," I tell them.

"Where did he take Garret?" a man asks from the back of the crowd.

"I don't know. He opened a door that I think might go to the old prison wing. The side of the resort that's not renovated yet." I don't mention the fact that Garret got locked in that wing just yesterday. I need their sympathy, not their accusations. "I tried to follow, but the door was locked. I pounded on the door as hard as I could, but no one answered."

"What makes you think he might be dead?" Pat asks.

I swallow past the lump forming in my throat. "He might be still alive, I don't know, but if he is, I can promise you that it didn't look good," I say, struggling to maintain my composure.

The murmurs grow louder. A ripple of unease spreads throughout the room. Miles steps to the front of the crowd and raises both hands. "Everybody, calm down. It's probably just Bruce. I've known him for a very long time. Yes, he's intimidating, but he's no killer. He's a teddy bear who wouldn't hurt a fly."

"You didn't see what I saw," I spew.

"I know what you think you saw," he says to me patronizingly. "But there could be some other explanation."

I sneer at him. "What do you know? You're the person who has now allowed two people to be killed or injured on your watch. You have no idea what's going on."

The crowd murmurs in agreement.

"Please, everyone," Miles responds, "we can't jump to conclusions. We need to stay together and stay calm. We'll figure this out."

"While you're in here staying calm, people are out there dying," I exclaim.

Sarah pipes up. "Do you think Bruce could have killed Kora?"

"No, of course not," Miles says as he vigorously shakes his head. "This is all ridiculous."

But the murmurs spread throughout the crowd once again as the realization that a potential killer might be amongst us sets in. The air is tinged with palpable fear. Miles's efforts to calm the group fall on deaf ears. Instead, panic rises, threatening to boil over.

I feel a firm hand on my shoulder and turn to see Dr. Callaway standing behind me, an earnest look on her face.

"Amelia, are you absolutely certain about what you saw?"

I nod, affirming. "Yes, at the very least, Garret was injured and passed out, but I touched his hand. If he was alive, he wouldn't have been that cold. When I first came into the room, Bruce was standing over him menacingly. He had to have done it."

Dr. Callaway sighs, rubbing her temples. "If that's true, then Garret needs help. If he's still alive, he's going to need me to help him, but, we can't just go rushing over there if Bruce is dangerous, we need a plan."

I nod enthusiastically. "What did you have in mind?"

Dr. Callaway continues. "Obviously, we need to go find him, but I'm not sure that splitting up is the best decision either. Right now, we have the advantage because of our numbers. Unless he has weapons, then we have the upper hand as long as we stick together."

"But we can't just stay here either," I say. I shudder at the thought of what might be happening to Garret. "We need to find him and rescue him." The weight of everyone's gaze is on me once again, suspended in anticipation.

"What do you think we should do?" asks the small blonde woman.

"We need to set a trap," Pat suddenly says, breaking the silence.

Dr. Callaway looks at him quizzically. "A trap?"

Pat nods with determination. "We have to make Bruce believe we're unaware of what's happening. Meanwhile, a group of us will be ready to confront him when he least expects it."

Miles looks increasingly agitated. "This isn't necessary," he says. "I know Bruce. He didn't do this."

Pat turns to him. "You really think you're competent to make a decision like this? Look at what's happened on your watch. One person is dead for sure and another one possibly is too. I don't think you get to say what is or is not necessary right now."

Miles shuts his mouth in shame and retreats to the back of the crowd. I almost feel sorry for him for half a second, but then think better of it. If he'd done a better job of vetting his employees, we wouldn't even be here.

"We can't risk losing another life," I say, feeling the weight of tears in my eyes. "Garret is out there still and he might still be alive. We need to send a group of us to go find him."

Voices rise to a dull roar as the realization of what we're about to do fills the room. I raise my hand. "Everybody, quiet. I have an idea." The crowd hushes. It is so silent in the room that we can hear the sounds of the snow outside softly patting against the windows.

Before I can speak, the double doors on the side of the room bang open. The crowd screams in fear as a tall figure walks into the banquet hall.

37

AMELIA

"That's him," the blonde woman screams.

Bruce walks confidently into the room, his broad frame dwarfing a dazed and bandaged Garret beside him. The room is thick with tension, the kind that seeps into your bones and sets every nerve on edge.

I rush to Garret's side. "Garret, are you okay?" He nods, but doesn't speak. I wrap my arms gingerly around him, but he doesn't hug me back.

I step back and look at Bruce. "What happened to him?"

"Not sure. All I know is I was sitting in the lobby and the next thing I know, he comes crawling over to my desk, looking like he's about to die."

"How could something like this just happen to him? Someone had to have done it," I say accusingly to Bruce.

"What are you trying to say? All I did was help him, in spite of how nasty he's been to me the entire time he's been here."

"But I saw you standing over him in the lobby as if you had just knocked him down," I challenge.

"Lady, I had to pick your husband up off the ground. Of

course, I was standing over him. If you don't believe me, check the recordings. It's my understanding that the video cameras are working again," Bruce responds as the crowd murmurs.

"Where did he come from?" Pat asks.

"I think he came from outside. Not quite sure. I had my headphones on and I was... preoccupied," Bruce replies.

All eyes turn to Garret.

He takes a deep breath and speaks. His voice sounds like gravel. "I got caught in the blizzard. I almost died out there. Bruce here took care of me, bandaged me up. I think I'm going to be okay," Garret explains.

Relief floods my body, followed by anger. "Are you really that stupid, Garret? What were you trying to do?"

"I don't know. Just get away from here. You should have seen how these people were attacking me. They think I killed Kora," Garret looks at me pleadingly. He's begging me to believe him.

I stare at him, my arms crossed. "You really have no idea what happened to Kora?" I whisper.

He shakes his head weakly. "No, I don't. I just got so tired of everybody accusing me that I left. It's a miracle I found my way back here. By the time I got to Bruce, I could barely stand up. I must have banged my head when I fell." His voice begins to fade as he struggles to stay conscious.

The crowd asks questions in rapid succession, all focused on Bruce. He puts his hands up, trying to ward them off.

"Is he telling the truth?"

"Did you see him come in from outside?"

"Was he really about to die?"

Bruce stands there silently, looking like a deer caught in the headlights. A man's voice breaks through the crowd. "He could have easily killed Garret, but he didn't. Instead, he bandaged him up and brought him back here. Doesn't that point to his innocence in the murder of Kora?"

The crowd murmurs as everyone ponders the question.

Sarah pipes up. "If it wasn't Bruce, then that means it was one of us." A hushed silence fills the room. Several people look at each other warily while several other eyes glare at Garret.

Miles steps to the front of the room. "Please, please, there's no reason to speculate any of this. We don't even know that this was foul play. Kora could have died of natural causes. I implore you to reserve your judgment until we know more information."

"What are you talking about?" Pat says with an angry scowl on his face. "Stop trying to cover up the truth."

The crowd gasps.

"I don't know what you're talking about," Miles stammers.

"Yes, you do," Pat accuses. "My wife told me that when she examined the body, it was obvious it was foul play and that you begged her to keep it a secret. Why?"

All eyes turn to Dr. Callaway. She nods. "Kora was most definitely murdered," she states, her voice unwavering. Then she looks at Miles. "It wasn't right for us to cover it up. People need to know the truth. I can't continue to stand by and pretend like this didn't happen. Someone here murdered Kora."

I look around again to gauge everyone's reactions. Panic rises amongst the group and the trust that had been building over the last few hours begins to disintegrate. Couples look at each other, wondering if it was one of them. Friends step away from each other, uncertain if their new friendship is based on a lie.

"Look at yourselves," Miles says. "This is exactly what I was trying to prevent. Now you're all panicking and worried that the person you're standing next to could be a killer. It's not like we can just leave this resort right now. We literally have nowhere to go in this blizzard. So yes, I lied about the nature of Kora's death when I said we weren't fully sure it was foul play. But it was for a good purpose," Miles says defensively.

Pat stares at him. "That's pretty convenient, Miles, making it so only you and my wife were the only ones who knew that Kora was killed. What if it was you and you've been spending these past few hours hiding the evidence? We know you haven't been in the banquet hall with us the whole time. You went off with those two to the generator," he says, pointing at me and Sarah. "But were you with them the entire time?"

I shake my head. "No, he wasn't. He left just after we got started and never came back."

"See, that proves my point," Pat says. "You could be the suspect here. How do we know that you haven't gone into her room during this time and removed objects that incriminate you? It's time we all start telling the truth. And that includes you, Miles."

"I didn't hurt Kora," Miles protests. "I promise you," he says, anguish evident on his face.

I look over at Garret and it looks like he's about to pass out. I wrap his arm around my shoulder to support his weight and then I look at the crowd. Several of them are talking to each other angrily.

"Everyone, please listen to me," I say as loudly as I can. Slowly, the crowd stops talking and looks towards me. "I know it's scary. One of us could be the killer, but they're not going to do anything in front of all of us. So, we're safe if we all stick together."

I look around and see several people nodding their heads in agreement, while others shake their heads in frustration.

I continue. "We also don't want another person wandering outside, trying to get away from the angry mob. It's best for us just to hold off and wait for detectives to get here. We need to force ourselves to stop jumping to conclusions. Anything we assume now is just speculation and if we're not careful, we're going to accuse the wrong person."

"She's right," Sarah pipes up. "We can't be falsely accusing each other of murder."

"I know my husband is pretty rude and difficult to get along with sometimes." I glance at Garret and he's staring at me with a shocked look on his face. "It's true, Garret," I say before returning to the crowd. "But he's not a killer. I don't think I've ever even seen him hurt a fly in his life. He almost died tonight trying to get away from all of you. This has to stop."

Murmurs of agreement ripple through the crowd, almost drowned out by a few loud voices of opposition.

"I agree with her," Sarah says. "We've got to stop accusing each other until we know the facts. Let's just try to get some sleep or something."

The weight of Garret's body grows heavier and I struggle to keep him upright. His eyes roll to the back of his head and his head lolls to the side.

"Someone, please help," I yell. "I can't hold him up much longer."

38

GARRET

I slowly come to, my head throbbing and my heartbeat echoing painfully in my temples. My hands and feet ache. My eyes flutter open and shut, the dim light from the room stabbing at them, forcing them closed. I groan. Where am I?

I try to remember the events of the past few hours. I struggle at first, only remembering bits and pieces. Suddenly, everything comes rushing back to me all at once. Oh no, Kora. The memory sears my chest, its pain outweighing that of all my other injuries.

I allow myself to drift to memories of Kora and I inwardly grieve for a few moments, desperately wanting to go back to sleep to avoid the pain.

Voices erupt around me, pulling me to the present. "I think he's awake," I hear someone say.

A gentle hand touches my arm and I force my eyes to open. Dr. Callaway sits in front of me, her stethoscope held to my chest. Her other hand lightly touches my forehead.

"How are you feeling?" She asks.

"Terrible," I say, my voice barely coming out in a whisper.

She nods. "That's to be expected. You got very lucky out there. It seems like you got inside before your hands and feet were completely frostbitten. You do have a little bit of frostnip on your toes and superficial frostbite on your fingers, but those should heal. Looks like you managed to keep your face covered up for the most part, so it looks okay too."

I nod. "I wasn't a complete idiot out there," I laugh slightly and then groan as the movement sends pain through my entire body.

I look around at where I'm sitting. I'm on one of the couches in the corner of the banquet hall. Several people are huddled around me, some of their eyes filled with concern, but many others are filled with questions. . . so many questions. I look around and realize that I'm not even sure I have the answers to any of them.

"I think he's going to be alright," the doctor says, pulling back. "He just needs some rest to fully recover."

"Thank you," Amelia says, sitting next to me. "You scared me," she says, her look seeming genuine.

I feel a pang of guilt. "I'm so sorry," I whisper.

"What were you thinking, Garret?" She asks, anger returning to her face. "You left just because people were asking you questions?"

"It's not that simple," I reply. "They weren't just asking me questions, Amelia. They were accusing me of murder."

My head throbs and I can barely see straight, but I know I have to give her the answers she's seeking. She deserves some explanation.

"So you felt walking in a blizzard was the right idea?" She asks, shaking her head.

"I know it was stupid. I should have never done it, but I felt like I had no choice. I believed it was the only way I was going to survive this weekend. It really felt like they were going to kill me, Amelia," I explain.

"You're an idiot, Garret," she says sharply. "If you had just stayed with the group, nobody was gonna kill you. They wouldn't risk getting caught in front of all of us."

"I had to... I just needed..." My voice is shaky, the words slipping away before I can grasp them.

Pat impatiently cuts in. "Needed what? To escape getting caught for murdering Kora?" He asks.

I wince as the reality of what's been happening hits me like a sledgehammer. The woman I love is dead and the woman I used to love is sitting here next to me, surrounded by a group of people who believe I'm a murderer. I have to get them off my back. They're never going to believe I'm innocent. I have to figure out a way to get them to start looking into somebody else.

I glance at Bruce, who is sitting across the room and before I even know what's happening, lies begin spilling out of my mouth. "Bruce," I croak, my dry throat making it hard to speak. "When I left the banquet hall, he... he approached me. He told me things about Kora." I feel a slight hint of guilt. The lies I'm telling could potentially hurt Bruce, but I'm not so sure that's a bad thing. There's something off about that guy. Besides, I need this group of jackals to stop looking into me and leave me alone.

The group exchanges worried glances.

Pat's brow furrows. "What did he tell you exactly?" He asks.

My words come out haltingly as I make them up on the fly. "He hinted at knowing something about Kora's death, something he wasn't willing to share with the rest of us. He also said he knew I was being accused and that he could help me find a way out. . ." I let the sentence hang, unable to articulate or come up with a valid excuse. Let them think what they want.

"Why would Bruce send you out into the storm like that?" Miles asks.

I glance over at Bruce, sitting on the other side of the room, his arms crossed, staring out the window. "I don't know. Maybe he was trying to kill me too."

Murmurs erupt in the small group surrounding me. The guilt returns, but I quickly shove it down. Maybe he didn't tell me about Kora, but I know if people look into him, they're going to find he has secrets. And maybe, just maybe, one of those secrets will take the suspicion off of me.

Miles pipes up once again, the consummate voice of reason. "It's obvious we do not know what happened here in the last twenty-four hours and we're never going to figure it out by making guesses and accusations. We need to stop all of this," he says. "I don't want anyone else getting hurt."

The group grumbles, but reluctantly agrees.

"Fine," Pat says. "I won't go over there and attack him, but you better believe, when given the chance, I'm going to ask him some hard questions. All we want is the truth."

Miles nods. "Just go easy on people, please, until the authorities arrive," he begs.

"I give you no promises," Pat says.

Relief floods my body. The identification of another suspect lifts the pressure from my back and I can feel myself relaxing and fading back into darkness.

"Help me lay him down," I hear Amelia say. I feel several hands around my upper body as they slowly lower me to the couch. A blanket is placed on me and I drift into a dark, dream-filled sleep.

39

KORA (PAST)

"Great rehearsal today, guys," I say to my band as I pack up my stuff and prepare to leave the studio space. We have a few high-profile gigs coming up that could really change things for us. So, we've been spending a few extra hours practicing every week.

"Running to your man?" the drummer asks, giving me a smirk.

I chuckle. "He's not my man anymore, remember?"

"Right," she says, disbelieving me.

"But no, he's not in town. Just have to head home to run some errands before the weekend."

"Have fun," she says.

"See you guys Friday night," I respond. I wave my hand and leave the room. As I walk down the stairs, I shake my head. It's been two weeks since Garret gave me that necklace. We're not officially back together, but we've been basically texting nonstop every day.

I haven't seen him since then. That concerns me a little. When I ask, he just says that he's busy with work and that he'll figure out a way to get back here more regularly, like he used to. I guess we'll see. I refuse to get back together with him until he has squared things with Amelia. I don't want him to just abandon her for me, so I guess I have to be patient.

My phone buzzes in my purse. I grab it and notice a new text message from Garret. Seeing a message from him still makes my heart flutter. My body's response is kind of ridiculous and semi-embarrassing. I don't check it right away, instead I walk to a nearby cafe before reading it. Usually, one message leads to an entire conversation and I can't be risking my life like that while I'm walking home.

I open the door to the coffee shop and the aroma of freshly brewed coffee fills the air. The warm oak tables and concrete floor give it a rustic yet modern feel. I order my usual sixteen-ounce soy latte, then make my way to a table on the far side of the room and sit before pulling out my phone and reading the text.

Baby. I miss you, it reads.

I quickly respond. *I miss you too. When will I see you next?*

Don't know. I'm hoping next week, he writes back.

I hope so, I say. *It's been too long. Did you figure out what you're going to do about your parents?*

I wait a long time before I see him typing a reply.

I've been thinking about that, he says. *I just need to get Amelia out of the picture.*

His words don't sit well with me. *What do you mean, out of the picture?* I quickly reply.

You know, if Amelia wasn't around then we wouldn't even have to worry about anything.

The implication of his words sends ice down my veins. Is he being serious? Is he really the type of man who would murder his wife for me? He can't possibly mean that. Have I misjudged his character that much? I have to know for sure before jumping to conclusions.

What do you mean, if she wasn't around, Garret?

Exactly what it sounds like. He texts back.

Fear grips my heart and I know in that instant I have to cut him off. There's a reason I ended things with Garret months ago — this is it. Whatever dark intentions he's hinting at, I cannot be a part of it. If he's thinking of getting rid of his wife for me, that's a line I can't cross. I won't be the reason someone loses their life.

I pick up the phone and call him. My hands are shaking, but I need to hear him say it out loud, whatever "it" is. He answers on the first ring, his voice too eager, too familiar. As the conversation unfolds, an icy dread creeps over me. By the time I hang up the phone, there's no more room for doubt. I can't do this. I can't stay.

With a deep breath, I type my final message: *This is it, Garret. We're done. I don't know exactly what you're planning to do to your wife, but I want no part of it. It's clear now that you don't know how to do the right thing. I need someone with integrity and that's not you. Goodbye.*

I hesitate, my thumb hovering over the send button. Maybe I misunderstood him. Maybe when he said he was going to get rid of her, he meant divorce, not something worse. But even so, the way he talks, it feels dangerous, like he's ready to cross lines no one should. Whether he means to ruin her in court or something more final, neither option is forgivable. She doesn't deserve this.

The realization hardens my resolve. I hit *send* and immediately see the three familiar dots appear. He's already typing back, probably panicking, wondering where he went wrong. But it's too late. I need to protect myself and maybe, by walking away, I'll protect her too.

I pull up Garret's contact on my phone and block him. Relief floods through me, but it's fleeting. A new notification pings from one of my social media accounts. My stomach twists. It's him.

Kora, don't do this to me. Please. I love you. Why are you leaving me like this?

I block him again, heart pounding. For the next several minutes, I go through every account I have, methodically blocking him from every corner of my life. The weight lifts slightly with each block, but a lingering sadness remains.

I loved him. A part of me still does. That's the truth I can't deny. It's going to take time to let go of the future I imagined with him — a future I thought we could build together. I allowed myself to dream, to believe he'd find a way to be with me without leaving destruction in his wake. I thought he'd come back ready to make it work. But now, every hope I had feels like a lie.

I stand from the table, leaving my latte untouched. I'm not in the mood for it anymore. The noise of the coffee shop feels distant, like the static hum of a radio I'm no longer tuned into. I walk slowly to the door, the weight of what just happened settling deep in my bones.

As I push the door open, the cool air outside hits me like a jolt. I pause for a moment, realizing how different I feel from the person I was when I walked in. In the span of a few minutes, my life has flipped upside down in ways I never saw coming.

I step out into the street, feeling the unfamiliar sensation of both grief and freedom. Moving forward won't be easy, but at least now I know — there's no going back.

40

AMELIA (PRESENT)

The morning light begins to stream through the big windows in the banquet hall. I grab an extra pillow and lightly place it over my head. The wind howls outside, picking up the snow from the ground and blowing gusts of it around in an ominous swirling motion. I can't believe Garret went out in that. What was he even thinking?

A row of pine trees less than ten feet away from the window sways in the wind, rocking back and forth as if in a dance. I watch their movement in awe. Such solid and seemingly immovable objects look like they're made of wet spaghetti.

"You can't sleep either, huh?" Garret says from his couch.

We pulled the two couches together before trying to sleep last night so that they were facing each other, allowing us to talk quietly without anyone else hearing.

I shake my head. "Not really. I think it's a combination of the light coming in through the window and all the other things racing through my mind."

He nods. "I should be passed out right now, but I can't sleep either."

He's quiet for a few minutes; it's as if he's trying to decide whether or not to say something. He finally speaks. "What do you think Bruce meant when he mentioned the security cameras were on again?"

I hesitate. I know exactly what he meant, but I don't know if I should tell Garret that I'm the one who turned them on. In the past, I would have told him everything, but now I'm not sure I know who he is anymore or if I can trust him. I eventually decide to keep it to myself. "I don't know. There are cameras everywhere in this building," I say, nodding to one in the corner of the room. "They must still be working, even though a lot of the power is out."

"Huh," Garret says quietly. "Good to know."

The wind outside picks up even more, rattling the windows. Suddenly, a loud cracking sound pierces the room. I sit up and look around. Everyone else still seems to be sound asleep.

I look out the window and watch in horror as a giant pine tree falls towards the window in what seems like slow motion. "Look out!" I scream as I get up and scramble away from the window as fast as I can. The tree crashes into the window, shattering the glass and leaving a gaping hole in its wake. It hits the ground with a resounding thud. The impact sends a shudder through the entire room.

Snow flurries from the outside rush in through the open space, quickly filling the room with tiny white flecks of snow. People all throughout the room scream as panic rises. "We could have died," a woman says across the way. Thankfully, it seems like the tree landed in a part of the room where no one was sitting or sleeping, but it's hard to tell what's underneath the tangled heap of branches and destroyed tables.

Miles rushes to the microphone. "Please. Everyone, stay calm." But his words fall on deaf ears. The panic in the room is palpable as everybody contemplates what to do next. This was supposed to be our safe space from the storm and the cold, but there's no fixing that hole. In a few moments, this room is going to become unbearably cold.

I look for Garret in the chaos. Where is he? I scan the faces in the crowd around Miles and don't see him. I walk over to the couch he slept on. The blanket he was using is bunched up on the end of the couch, but there's no sign of Garret. Frustration fills me. Why did he leave again? Where did he go this time?

41

AMELIA

This is just like Garret. Even after getting lost in a blizzard, he still hasn't learned his lesson. I shake my head in disbelief. How can he be so dense? All he has to do is stay here and he doesn't look suspicious. If the people find out he's gone, I'm pretty sure there's no way I'm going to be able to keep the mob from refocusing on him as Kora's murderer.

I have to find him before anyone figures out he's missing. There's no way I'm wandering these halls again, all by myself. There has to be a better way. I look around the room and try to gain inspiration. In the far corner of the room, I spot Sarah standing with a group of hotel employees and a lightbulb goes off in my head. The security cameras should all be on by now. If I can somehow convince Miles to let me look at them, maybe I can find Garret before he does something stupid.

I scan the room and find Miles over by the couches, surrounded by a group of angry guests. I walk over to them and stand in the back.

"When will the power come back on?" An angry man asks.

Miles responds. "I really wish I knew the answer to that, but I'm in the same position as you are. I'm sure they're working on it as we speak."

"What are you doing about figuring out who the murderer is?" A woman asks.

"Ma'am, like I've said before," Miles continues, "it's not our place to be detectives. I'm going to wait for the police to get here so they can do their job. In the meantime, I suggest you all stop speculating."

I inwardly laugh. There's no way these people are going to stop talking about it. They all believe that they're master sleuths of some kind and can figure this whole thing out on their own. By the time the police arrive, they'll have concocted some crazy theory that they are one hundred percent convinced is the most logical explanation.

I stand at the back of the crowd as they continue to ask Miles question after question. Many of them have already been answered at least once. Miles patiently responds; even in this high-stress scenario, he has maintained his composure. I'm impressed.

I wait until their questions die down before walking up to him and placing my hand on his shoulder. "Miles, could I have a word with you privately, please?"

His eyes, bloodshot and weary, meet mine. "Sure," he says. We walk about ten to fifteen feet away from the group.

"What's going on?" Miles asks.

"Garret's missing again," I whisper.

"Can you repeat that? I can't hear you."

I sigh and raise my voice slightly. "Garret's missing again."

"What?" A voice says from behind. I turn to see Pat

standing behind us, a scowl on his face. "Your husband is gone again? If that's not evidence that he's guilty of Kora's death, I don't know what is."

"He probably just went to the bathroom," I say, trying to downplay the situation.

"Right," Pat retorts. "After we were all told to go in pairs, he decides to go alone. What gives him that right?"

"I don't know. He doesn't really listen very well, obviously," I reply, frustration evident in my voice.

"How do we know he's not tampering with the girl's body right now, trying to get rid of any evidence that he had anything to do with her death?" Pat presses.

I rub my temples, exasperated. How could you be such an idiot, Garret? Here I go again, trying to defend him when all he's done for me over the last several years is lie and disrespect me. I'm only doing this because I don't want him to go down for murder.

Miles interrupts. "The security cameras are now on. We should be able to easily figure out where he is."

I look at him pleadingly. "Would you go with me and help me find him?"

He nods. "I think it's best for everyone to know his location. If he's in Kora's room, that will be a good indication that he's the killer and we may be able to contain him or something until the police arrive."

"That's right," Pat says, nodding in agreement. "You better do something like that. I'm tired of him continuing to get away while the rest of us are sitting here following orders," he says, exasperated.

"Alright, let me grab my things and we'll leave," Miles says to me.

"Before you go, Miles, what's your plan about the big

hole in the window? It's getting really cold in here," Pat inquires.

Miles runs his fingers through his hair, clearly stressed. "Yeah, I know. I'm thinking we're going to have to relocate to another room in the building. I'm just not sure where yet."

"Well, you better figure it out. People aren't going to survive long in this," Pat warns.

Miles nods in agreement. "When I come back, I'll have a plan to get us out of here. It's obvious we're not fixing that window anytime soon."

I look around the banquet hall. People are huddled under blankets, many of them piled two to three on a couch, trying to keep warm. "I don't think we have a lot of time. They're not going to last very long in here."

"Well, then let's hurry," he replies. "We'll go to the security room, check the camera footage, figure out where Garret is and then come back here to move all of us to a new location."

"Where do you think we'll go?" I ask.

He shakes his head. "I'm not sure, but I think I can turn the power on in the hotel room block. It takes up more electricity, so the generator won't last as long, but we don't have much choice."

I look around. "People would probably appreciate laying down in their beds again, too. I think that's a good idea."

"Hopefully, this blizzard stops soon," he says wearily.

I nod. "Hopefully, but it doesn't really look like that's going to happen anytime soon."

Pat, overhearing our conversation, chimes in impatiently. "Well, what are you guys doing just standing here?" He asks. "Hurry up and look at your footage so we can get out of here."

Miles nods and rushes over to his bag. He bends down to grab a pair of flashlights and as he does, I notice the corner of a picture poking out of his back pocket. I wonder what that is? It must be important enough for him to keep it with him.

I shake my head; it's none of my business. Right now, I just need to focus on finding Garret. I hope he hasn't done something stupid.

42

AMELIA

Miles walks quickly in front of me. He illuminates the hallway with his flashlight and leads us down the corridors towards the security room.

I follow close behind, shining my flashlight on his back.

"It's pretty creepy in here without any lights on," he says.

"Yeah, I wouldn't recommend anybody walk down here by themselves. I did it once and let's just say it's a little terrifying," I respond.

"I'm not sure why the owners of this place decided to turn a prison into a hotel. They could have just demolished the thing and rebuilt it, putting a brand-new resort in its place. I know they couldn't have saved money by keeping it standing. I've seen the construction bills." He says, shaking his head. "But we have had a lot of interest from around the world. There are some weird people out there who find this intriguing."

"It's definitely a good marketing ploy," I say, "but it is kind of weird sleeping in a jail cell."

We reach the security room. Miles puts his hand into his

back pocket to take out his key card. "The generator powers this room so it can remain locked and secure, even in a power outage."

As he pulls his hand out of his pocket, the picture I saw peeking out of it earlier comes out and falls to the ground. I shine my flashlight on it.

"You dropped something," I say, picking it up. As soon as I do, ice runs through my veins. In the picture, Miles looks to be about twenty pounds lighter and his hair is much longer. Kora is cuddled up next to him on what looks to be a dorm room bed, his arms wrapped around her. He turns towards me and I look up at him. His face is drained of its color.

"What is this, Miles?"

"It's nothing. Give it back," he says, taking a step towards me.

I back up. "This looks like an older picture. How long have you known her?" I ask incredulously.

He takes another step forward and quickly grabs the photo from my hand. "It's not what it looks like," he says defensively.

"Then what is it, Miles? It's obvious you've known her for a really long time and not just as friends."

He shakes his head. "It was a long time ago, okay? We dated back in college, that's it."

"And you just happened to find her and ask her to come sing here?" I shake my head. "That's too much of a coincidence, Miles."

"No, she's always been an amazing singer. And when we needed entertainment, she was the first person that came to my mind."

"So you brought your ex here to sing at the resort and

you didn't think it was relevant for the rest of us to know that? Especially after she's found dead?"

"No, because it doesn't mean anything. When we broke up, it was amicable and we've been friends ever since. I would never do anything to hurt her."

I shake my head. Does everybody have secrets around here? It's starting to feel like there's no one I can trust. "How do I know that we're not coming into the security room right now so that you can erase the footage of you killing Kora?" I question. "I don't know anything about your security system. It would be really easy for you just to delete a few files with a few strokes of the keyboard. If I hadn't seen that picture, I would have never even known to watch you and make sure you weren't erasing evidence."

"I swear, I'm just here to look for Garret. I want to find the killer as much as you do," he says, swiping his key card and opening the door. "Come on, let's just get this over with. The more time we argue out here in the hallway, the longer Garret has to do whatever he's doing and disappear before we find him."

It dawns on me that I am alone now with Miles. How could I be so stupid? I try to not panic and talk myself down. Any number of the workers at this resort could have some history with Kora. It makes sense that she would at least know some of them. Maybe it's not a big deal that she knew Miles. I walk into the room behind him, leaving the door open.

Miles walks towards the computer that contains the security footage. I can see that my attempts to divert power to the computer seem to have worked. The computer screen is on, but locked. The username is pre-populated, but the password field is blank. Miles types in a password and the screen comes to life.

After a few seconds, the live camera streams from each of the cameras around the compound fill the screen.

I walk up next to him and begin to scan each one slowly, hoping to find Garret somewhere on the cameras.

"You know I'm going to have to tell everyone," I say to Miles. "It's not fair for Garret to be the only suspect here when you also knew her."

He looks at me, fear in his eyes. "You can't do that, Amelia."

"I have to. An investigation would not be authentic if all suspects weren't brought forward," I insist.

I watch as panic fills his face and he rushes to the open door and closes it. "I can't let you do that. I can't let you out of here if you're going to tell people that I knew her. We were keeping it secret for a reason," he says, anger filling his face.

"What are you doing, Miles? Let's talk about this."

He shakes his head. "I can't have people find out. Please, Amelia, they'll never understand. They'll crucify me."

43

MILES

I stand in front of the door, blocking Amelia's escape, my mind racing with thoughts of desperation. How could I have been so careless as to drop that picture? Until now, everything had been perfect; nobody, not even the staff, had figured out that Kora and I had known each other before. We kept our distance, only talking to each other in the privacy of our own rooms. I should have put that picture away the moment I took it. I should have hidden it in my room, not in my back pocket. What was I thinking?

In the chaos of everything, I let my guard down and now this woman in front of me could ruin everything. "I can't have people find out. Please, Amelia, they'll never understand. They'll crucify me," I implore her.

"It wouldn't be that bad," she responds. "Yeah, they're going to ask you questions and be suspicious of you, but nobody's going to do anything to you."

I shake my head vehemently. "You don't understand. I'm the most likely suspect here, especially considering our history. I know that, but I didn't do it. I swear."

She crosses her arms, skepticism written on her face. "I

have a hard time believing that, Miles. You were so desperate to get those security cameras back up and running. It's hard for me to think that it wasn't just so you could delete those files."

I vigorously shake my head. "No, that wasn't it. I swear. I wanted to see who went into her room and killed her. I wanted the evidence. I could have never hurt her."

"So, you were in love with her?" Amelia asks.

I lower my head; that's probably an understatement. If there's something beyond love, that's how I felt for Kora. There hasn't been a day in ten years that I haven't thought about her and everything I lost the day we broke up. She became the perfect woman in my mind and I idolized her, but I can't tell Amelia that. It will make me look insane. So I say nothing and my silence is as good as an answer.

"Of course you were. Everyone's in love with her, I guess," she says bitterly. "First you and now Garret. I wonder how many other men she had on the hook?"

"So it's true?" I ask quietly, not sure if I want to know the answer. "She and Garret were seeing each other?"

She shrugs and sighs. "You saw the look on his face when he saw her. Everyone did. And his actions have been so shady since the moment we arrived. I think it's safe to say that something was going on there."

A sharp pain erupts in my chest. It's not like I was naive enough to think she didn't date other people since we ended things, but since she got here, I've been able to pretend that there's no one else and that I had a real shot. I guess maybe I was wrong, but now it doesn't even matter because she's gone. I have to focus now on making sure I make it out of here without going to jail for her murder.

My mind races. What do I do next? I can't let her go back and tell people. I scan the room and spot a pile of cords in the corner. I could tie her up, but I'm not sure that I'm willing to cross that line. Plus, it would be a battle and I could get hurt in the process. I continue looking and spot a door open in the corner of the room — a storage closet. If I could somehow get her in there, then I could keep her there until the police arrive and conduct the real investigation.

In a split decision, I rush forward toward Amelia and use my weight to push her toward the open door. She loses her balance and stumbles backward, nearly falling to the ground. I grab hold of her tightly to prevent her from falling, then shove her into the room, quickly closing the door behind her before she can stand and fight back. As soon as the door is closed, I turn the key and lock her in. I remove the key from the handle and put it in my pocket.

My heart is pounding and my breathing is ragged.

She bangs on the door and yells loudly, her voice muffled by the thickness of the wood. "Let me out, Miles. This is not okay. You can't trap me in here."

"I'm sorry, Amelia," I say, pressing my face close to the door, my voice laced with guilt. "I can't let you jeopardize everything, not when we're so close to finding the truth."

Her muffled screams and shouts are relentless as she pounds harder on the door. I lean against it and take a deep breath, my mind swirling with emotion. Locking her up was not part of the plan, but I had no choice.

If the rest of them knew about my relationship with Kora, it would divert their attention from the real killer and I can't let that happen. I'll come back here and let her out as soon as the police arrive and the real investigation can begin, but until then, it's safer for me that she's here.

44

MILES (PAST)

This opening weekend couldn't be going any better. The guests were happy at dinner tonight. They loved hearing Kora sing and were enamored with the food, except for that guy, Garret, who left in the middle of everything. From the look on his face, I could have sworn he knew Kora. I shake my head. It would be too much of a coincidence, right?

I try to push the thought aside, but it won't leave me. What if he's her lover? They could have been having an affair. Would Kora have told me? I try to convince myself she would, but I'm not so sure. I haven't had a chance to tell her how I feel yet and for the most part, we've been keeping our distance for the sake of optics, but she would have told me if she had a boyfriend, wouldn't she?

Doubt seeps into my mind. I know that she's dated people over the last ten years; I'm not ignorant. And it's not like we've really had a chance to sit down and talk about what we've done during that time. The only way for me to know for sure is to talk to her. I need to set the record straight, so I know where I stand.

It's late, but I'm sure she's still awake. She always gets this post-performance high that keeps her awake for a few hours after she has a gig.

I walk towards her room down a cold corridor. I shiver – we really have to figure out a way to get heat to these parts of the resort; it feels almost as cold in here as it is outside.

When I reach her room, I knock on the door – no answer. I wait several more seconds before knocking again, but still, there's no answer. Where could she be? Maybe she's with Garret. The thought forms a pit in my stomach. What if they're in there right now and don't want to respond because they don't want me to come in?

Irrational thoughts flood my brain and panic rises inside of me. I need to know the truth. I know I shouldn't do it, but I pull my keys out of my pocket and find the master key. I know this is an invasion of her privacy, but I have to know the truth. I slide the key into the lock and unlock the door. I turn the handle slowly, as if doing it quieter will make a difference.

In a moment of panic, I swing the door open. The room is dark. Initially, I can't see anything, but as my eyes adjust, I discern a form lying on the ground. My throat constricts and I stop breathing for several seconds. Is that Kora?

I hastily turn on the light, a stifled sob escaping my lips as the stark reality hits me. Lying in the middle of the floor is Kora, her body lifeless and pale. Every fiber of my being wants to scream, but I suppress it.

"No," I whisper, my voice trembling with disbelief. Maybe she's just passed out. Maybe I can still wake her up. I move closer to the body and tentatively reach out to touch her. Her body is as cold as it looks and I recoil, my hands trembling. She's dead, but how? I see no obvious wounds, but I'm no expert in that kind of stuff.

Thoughts of what happened to her are silenced as a wave of grief washes over me. I sink to my knees as despair threatens to overwhelm me. "Oh, Kora, what happened to you?" I can't believe she's actually gone. It feels like a cruel joke – the moment I finally have a chance to reconnect with the love of my life, she's gone.

I kneel on the floor next to her body and weep silently for what feels like hours. Eventually, the tears dry up and I stand, my rational mind beginning to take back over. I shouldn't be here. I had no valid reason to unlock her door except for jealousy. People are going to think I had something to do with her death if they found out that I was the one who discovered her; it looks too suspicious. I need to find someone else to be here with me when she's discovered.

Then it hits me. Maybe I can tell someone I'm worried about Kora and that she won't answer her phone. If I can convince them that something might be wrong, then maybe they'd be willing to come with me to check on Kora in case something's happened to her.

I turn off the light and quietly close the door behind me. If I do this right, no one will even know that I came in here alone and found her first. I walk down the corridor towards the guest rooms. As I'm walking down the hall, I look up and notice a flashing red light – a security camera. Crap. I forgot we had those everywhere in this resort. They were installed when this place was a prison and the resort owner wanted to keep them. That means there's a recording of me going into her room. I have to delete that footage somehow.

45

MILES (PRESENT)

I sit on my bed in my room, far away from the angry mob in the banquet hall and Amelia's screams in the security room closet. How did everything go so wrong? Before yesterday, I had been walking around so hopeful that Kora and I would eventually get back together.

That hope only intensified the weekend she came here to rehearse her set for opening weekend. I remember the day she arrived vividly. Even though I had seen her just a few weeks before, I still was overwhelmed by the sight of her.

THE MOMENT KORA saw me at the resort, her eyes lit up and she pulled me into a warm hug. We were alone at the time; the rest of the staff was busy preparing for the guests' arrival.

"I still can't get over this place," she said, her eyebrows raised.

I chuckled. "Yeah, it's not my cup of tea, but it seems like a lot of people are interested."

"Well, do you want to show me to my room?" She asked.

"Right this way," I said, gesturing towards the hallway off to the right.

I grabbed her bags and we walked together down the hallway. As we walked, we chatted with each other a little bit, flirting off and on. It almost felt just like the old days. I opened the door to her room and let her in. She turned on the light and stood in the middle of the room for several seconds, looking around.

"Everything okay?" I asked.

"It's a prison cell," she said.

I shook my head. "No, not exactly. This was a guard station. It's still a little industrial because we're not done with the interior decorating, but I think you're going to be impressed the next time you come."

She shrugged. "It's fine. It's just a place to sleep, right?"

I nodded. "This is going to be your room every weekend that you're here," I said. "You can make it as homey as you want."

She nodded and a small smile returned to her face. "Okay. Next time I come up here, I will bring some stuff with me. Maybe some pictures for that corkboard or something," she said, pointing to the board that had been hung on one of the walls.

"Great," I said. "I'm going to let you get settled in."

"Hey, Miles," she said, grabbing my hand. "I know that we agreed not to let anyone know we know each other, but I do want to spend time with you while I'm here."

Hope flooded my heart. "You do?"

She nodded and a small smile formed on her lips. "Yeah. We had a good thing going back in the day. And I don't know, maybe we can find our way back to what we were. No promises though, but it's a thought."

I gave her a big, toothy grin as I contemplated the idea of spending more time with her. It had been more than I had even been willing to hope for. "I'd like that."

"It may not be something that happens right away," she said, "I'm still trying to get over my last thing, but I'd love to spend time with you."

"I can make that happen," I said, grinning from ear to ear. "I'll come find you when it's time for practice."

Over the next several days, Kora and I spent hours together, laughing, remembering the past and enjoying each other's company. On her last day, she brought up one of the most painful memories in my life. We were lying on her bed together, looking at the ceiling. Our arms touched just slightly, sending tingles up my spine. I was enjoying just being close to her.

"Do you remember the day I left for L.A.?" She asked.

I nodded. "How could I forget?"

SUDDENLY, I was transported back ten years in my mind as I relived the moment that destroyed everything for me. Kora was in our bedroom hastily packing her things.

"You don't have to do this, Kora," I said.

"I do. I really do. You don't get it."

"Then explain it to me," I urged her.

She stopped and turned to me, tears streaming down her face. "I'm tired of working these dead-end jobs here in Seattle. It's just time for me to pursue my dreams, Miles."

"What, just because you got fired?"

Hurt spread across her face. "You think I'm not good enough to make it, don't you?"

"I didn't say that," I said, frustrated. "I'm just saying that when you left for work this morning, you weren't thinking about moving to L.A."

"I've always thought about moving to L.A. I just don't talk about it."

"Okay, fine, but why can't you just wait until we are both ready to go?"

"Because I just hit my breaking point. Every moment that I'm not down there, I'm not following my dreams. If you want to come with me, fine, but you're gonna have to meet me down there because I'm going now."

"How are you even going to get there, Kora?" My voice rose in frustration and her impulsiveness.

"I have a car, you know." She said angrily.

"You're gonna drive all the way to L.A. by yourself?"

She put her hands on her hips and glared at me. "So what?"

"Kora, that's not safe."

"You can't protect me from everything, Miles," she retorted angrily. "Do you know all of the people I'm going to come in contact with when I'm in L.A.? I don't even know where I'm living yet. You're not going to find any of this safe, but I'm doing it anyway. I'm just taking a leap," she said.

I shook my head. "You're really just going down there with no plan?"

"Yep," she said. "I've saved up a few thousand dollars. It should last me a little while while I try to figure things out."

"What about us?" I asked quietly.

Her face softened. "If you're not coming, I don't know if there should be an us anymore."

My heart sank. I had been afraid of this. I always knew that she wanted to pursue her dreams and I never really understood how or if I fit in them, but in that moment, it had been clear to me that I didn't.

"So we're breaking up?" I asked.

She nodded as the tears picked up steam. "I'm sorry, Miles. I do love you, but I have to do this for me. And I have to do it by myself."

"So you don't actually want me following you down to L.A.?"

"I don't think you'll actually do it. You love Seattle too much to leave it," she said sadly.

"What's wrong with loving Seattle?"

She walked over to me and wrapped her arms around me. "Don't hate me, Miles. Someday, when my music career is off and running, I'll come find you and we can see what we have," she said.

I just hugged her back, unable to speak.

THAT DAY WAS HARD, but eventually, we found each other again at this weird hotel.

I opened my eyes and found myself in the prison-resort with Kora lying next to me. "I guess this is the someday in the future we talked about when you left for L.A.," I said to her.

She grabbed my hand. "Let's get to know each other again and see what happens," she said.

THAT DAY, I was filled with hope and I was so happy. Today, sitting on my bed, I'm unsure of what I have to live for. I stare at the picture of me and Kora.

I grab my lighter out of my pocket and flick it on. I know

I have to get rid of any evidence that could make me out to be the killer. The yellow flame dances for a moment underneath the paper before it eventually catches on fire. The flames slowly consume our faces. The ashes float away into the room and my hope of a future with Kora dissolves with them.

46

AMELIA

I can't believe he trapped me in this storage closet. Desperation seizes me as I contemplate being stuck in here forever. What am I going to do?

I pound on the door, screaming until I'm hoarse, but it's no use. No one comes to my rescue. The storage closet door has a tiny window higher than I can reach. I look around the room and notice a stool folded up in the corner of the tiny room. I grab it and push it to the door.

I quickly glance around again, taking note of the other items in the closet. It seems to be one of those closets that has become the dumping ground for everything that doesn't have a place. From what I can tell, it's mostly a combination of tech and maintenance tools.

I climb up the stool and peek out the window. Inside the security room, the lights are still on, but there's no one to be seen. How am I going to get out of here? My heart starts to pound as panic sets in.

What if there's not enough oxygen in this room? How long can a person last in a room like this with no oxygen? My mind races with all the possibilities, settling on the worst ones. "Stop it. Get yourself together, Amelia," I whisper.

Suddenly, a figure appears in the hallway. He first peeks his head into the security room and then walks inside. It's Garret. What's he doing in here? Maybe he can save me.

I pound on the door as hard as I can. "Garret!" I yell. "Help me, please, Garret."

He stops and stares at the door. His face is expressionless, almost as if he's a zombie.

I pound even louder, hoping that my pleas will reach him, but instead of walking over to the door and helping me get out, he turns and walks out of the room. What in the world, Garret? Why would he ignore me and leave me in here like this? Maybe he couldn't hear me yelling. Deep down, I know that's not true. He heard me yelling and chose to ignore me, just like he's been ignoring me at home now for years.

I sink down the door and sit on the stool, placing my head in my hands. What am I going to do? I can't be stuck like this; I have to get out of here. It's clear I can't rely on anyone else to save me.

I've spent almost my entire life depending on other people. Garret and I got married so young. I barely had a chance to live on my own before we were living together. There's so much I haven't learned. I don't even know what half of these tools in this closet do. Garret always took care of that kind of stuff. Now, I'm stuck with no hope of anyone else coming to my rescue. I'm gonna have to figure out a way to get myself out.

47

AMELIA (PAST)

I close the book with a sigh. The silence in my bedroom feels heavier than usual. I glance at the clock — it's already nine. Time always seems to drag and race at the same time in this empty house.

I head to the kitchen, flipping off lights as I go, the house growing darker with each switch. The stillness follows me, pressing in from all sides. I pour myself a glass of wine, the sound of the liquid hitting the glass the only break in the quiet.

I never imagined my life turning out this way — spending so many nights alone, waiting for a husband who is rarely home. When Garret first started taking these trips to L.A., we talked every night. As soon as he finished work, he'd call without fail. He'd tell me about his meetings and the view from his hotel room and even though he was far away, I still felt connected to him.

But lately, the calls have dwindled. Now, I'm lucky if I hear from him once a week. Not for lack of trying, either. I send messages, leave voicemails — but more often than not, they go unanswered.

I sit at the kitchen island, swirling the wine in my glass, staring at the empty seat across from me. It feels like I'm holding onto a ghost of something that used to feel full and warm, but now only leaves me cold.

I sip the wine slowly, trying not to dwell on the ache in my chest. The kind of ache that comes when you realize the person you love most has slipped out of reach — and you have no idea how to get them back.

I dial Garret's number and put it on speakerphone. It rings twice before going to voicemail. Why is he sending me to voicemail all the time? I open the text messaging app.

Garret, call me. I haven't heard from you since the day you left and it's now Thursday. You could be dead for all I know. Of course, I know he's not dead; he just sent me to voicemail, but a little guilt trip doesn't hurt.

The message immediately shows as being read, but he does not respond. I can't keep doing this. I need real interaction — someone to share my thoughts and feelings with. Right now, they're just all bottled up inside of me and there are days when I feel like I'm about to explode.

I down my glass of wine, trying to drown this feeling of emptiness. I can't say it really helps, but it does dull it a bit, making it easier to cope with. I grab the bottle and pour myself another drink.

I turn on the TV and flip through the channels. It never seems like there's anything good on, or maybe it's just that I'm never really in the mood to watch anything these days. After watching a few cooking videos, I end up settling on a hidden camera show focused on catching cheaters. I look at my phone again. Still no messages. How could someone just abandon their marriage like this?

When he made the first trip to L.A., I was hesitant because it was so far, but he swore up and down it was just going to be a few days. That's it. And then he'd be right back here with me. True to his word, that first trip was only a few days, but then he went the next week and the week after and now it's been months.

He swears that he's making more money now that he's doing his business in California. I don't know for sure. I don't see his business account or anything like that, but our lifestyle hasn't changed.

I still drive the beat-up old sedan that I bought when we first started dating. While it was new to me then, it definitely wasn't a new car. By the time I got it, it already had one hundred thousand miles on it. It still runs, but it's definitely seen better days. The air conditioning doesn't work consistently and one of the windows doesn't roll down. If Garret's doing so well with his job in L.A. and considering his family is rich, you'd think he would do something about that, but no, he says we can't afford it.

There are also repairs on this house that need to be made. A couple of pieces of siding got damaged in a windstorm and need to be replaced. The faucet in the kitchen is leaking; it drips nonstop, nearly driving me crazy. Garret was always the one to fix those things. I suppose I could learn how to do it myself, but I don't want to have to. I want my husband here with me like he used to be.

I grab my phone and try Garret one more time. This time, it doesn't immediately go to voicemail and after the fourth ring, he finally picks up.

"Hello," he says.

"Garret, you answered," I say relieved.

"What do you want?" The coldness in his voice sends chills through my body.

"We just haven't talked since you left. It's like we're living separate lives," I admit, tears pricking my eyes. "I miss you. I miss us."

The other end of the line is silent for a few seconds before Garret responds. "Work's been hectic, you know how it is."

"So busy that you can't even bother to call me for a few minutes at night?"

"I've been taking clients out. You know I've got to wine and dine them to get their business."

"Garret, I just... I feel so alone. Even when you're here, to be honest," I say.

He doesn't respond. It's almost as if he doesn't care. Finally, he speaks up and changes the topic. "How is work?"

"Fine, we got some new chocolates in. So, same old stuff, I guess... When are you going to stop working in two cities?"

He takes a second to respond. He's probably surprised by my directness. "I don't have a choice, Amelia. This is where the work is," he says.

I shake my head. "We were doing just fine when you were here and not in L.A. You're not bringing home more money every week. So where's the money all going, Garret?"

"It's coming, I promise. I just have to build up this clientele," he says.

"Okay," I say skeptically. "If you really think that this is best for us, then fine."

"I promise, you'll see. Things are going to change."

"I need it to change," I say. "I have to get away from here. I need a break from everything. I think I'm gonna go to my sister's this weekend. I'll leave after you get home."

"Sounds good," he replies without hesitation.

I had hoped he would at least pretend like he cared that I was leaving. Deep down, I was really hoping he would beg me to stay to spend time with him, but he couldn't even be bothered to pretend to care. What happened to us? How did we end up so distant from each other?

"Amelia, I gotta go. My clients are waiting for me back at the table," he says.

I look at the clock. It's nine-thirty pm. "You're eating dinner this late?"

"That's how they do it here. Late dinners, even later drinks," he says. "If I want their business, I have to play their game."

I sigh. "Fine, go. I'll see you when you get home."

He doesn't even say goodbye before he hangs up the phone.

I set my phone down and stare at the TV without even really watching what's on it. Something strange is going on with Garret. This is not normal behavior. I need to figure out what it is.

48

AMELIA (PAST)

I sift through Garret's suitcase, pulling pairs of pants and shirts out of the main cavity of the bag and neatly placing them on the bed. He got home an hour ago and immediately went to the gym.

Normally, Garret unpacks his own bag, but I need the suitcase to go to my sister's, so I'm doing it for him. As soon as all the clothes are out of the suitcase, I glance around the room. Should I wash them for him or put them away? Then, reason strikes me upside the head. He can do it himself. I've been too accommodating for far too long. This weekend is about me.

I catch sight of the photograph of Garret and me on our wedding day proudly displayed on our dresser. The younger, happier version of us seems to mock me. That time almost feels like a dream. Were we ever that happy? Looking at our lives now, it's hard for me to believe that we ever really were. How did two people so happy get to this point? It feels almost like we're strangers now.

I walk over to the dresser and place the photo face down.

I don't need a reminder of what we once were. I don't even know if there's a way to fix it because I don't understand what's broken. It just feels like things changed overnight and I have no control.

I walk back over to the suitcase and unzip the inside pocket, pulling out a few wads of twenties I found stuffed inside. I grab the twenties and stuff them into my own pocket. I'm going to need a little spending money this weekend, right? He'll probably never even miss it. I feel around the pocket for anything left and my hand touches what feels like a small piece of paper. I pull it out. It's a sealed envelope. On the front of the envelope, in beautiful cursive, it says, *to my love.*

I momentarily stop breathing. What is this? Who wrote this for Garret? My heart pounds in my chest and my breath becomes shallow. I quickly slide my finger under the envelope flap and carefully open it. Inside is a letter written in the same beautiful cursive.

My dear Garret,

I hope you find this note sometime this weekend and it makes you smile. I want you to know that I love you so much. I'm so grateful that you have come into my life. I can't wait until we can be together full-time and make a family.

Love always,

Kora.

THE PIECE of paper falls out of my hand onto the bed. Who is this Kora? Is that what Garret's been doing this whole time? Having an affair? I thought he was just getting distant.

It didn't even dawn on me that he might be seeing somebody else. How naive could I possibly be? This explains everything — the unreturned phone calls, the weeks away — and I've just been letting it happen.

I notice something else inside the envelope. I pull it out; it's a photograph of Garret. His arm is wrapped around a tall, curly-haired woman, her head tilted back in laughter. There's a smile on her face that reminds me of the smiles I used to make when Garret and I first met. Impulsively, I rip the photograph in half.

How could he do this to me? Is he really planning on leaving me for her? Is he going to destroy everything we've worked so hard to build? The thought of it makes me sick to my stomach.

I continue yanking things out of the pockets in the suitcase and tossing them on the bed in an angry rage. In another pocket, I find a wad of receipts, each of them to some fancy restaurant in L.A., all billed for two.

My heart sinks even further with every piece of evidence I find. How long has this been going on? For weeks? Months? I can feel the walls closing in as a nauseating mixture of betrayal and grief courses through me. I thought this was just a rough patch between us, but this is something else entirely. I wasn't prepared for this.

As soon as the suitcase is empty, I look at the contents on the bed and then it hits me. I can't let him know that I know about all this until I figure out what I'm going to do. I need to have the upper hand.

I grab the note and the picture and place them in my pocket, being careful not to leave any pieces behind. It wasn't opened, so maybe he didn't even know it was there. Hopefully, he won't figure out it's missing. I neatly arrange everything else on the bed. I put the receipts in one of his pockets. Maybe he'll think he put them there for safekeeping; he doesn't have the greatest memory.

Once I'm satisfied that there's no lingering evidence of what I've found, I quickly fill the suitcase with my own clothes and toiletries. I'm so glad I decided to go away. I need this time to think and figure out what to do.

49

AMELIA (PAST)

Marigold's porch looks just as I remember it. Large pots of petunias grace both sides of the door. I slam the door behind me as I get out of the car.

Marigold steps out onto the porch, her eyes wide with surprise. "Amelia?" She asks, confused.

"Hi, Marigold," I say sheepishly.

"What are you doing here?"

"I just had to get away for the weekend and I didn't want you to say no, so I drove here without calling you."

She opens her arms wide. "Why? You know I would never say no to you."

I walk up to her and allow her to wrap her arms around me in a hug.

"Is everything okay?" She asks as she pulls away from me and looks me in the eyes.

I've never been able to lie to her. She's been more like a mother to me my whole life than a sister.

She was only four when I was born, but my parents were always so busy making sure their house was ready for the coming apocalypse that Marigold took on a lot of the parenting responsibilities, even though she was only a few years older than me.

When I was in elementary school, she made my lunches and made sure I had the right shoes for the weather. As I got older and she became old enough to drive, she took me to my activities. When I played basketball in middle school, it wasn't my mom or dad screaming for me on the sidelines. It was Marigold.

I remember the first time I got dumped. I was fourteen and thought that I was going to marry my boyfriend, Brad, someday. When he ended things with me, I was devastated. Marigold came to pick me up from the park where Brad had just told me he wasn't in love with me anymore. I tried so hard to hide my pain, but the moment I opened the door, she knew exactly what had happened.

Today is no different.

"What did he do?" She asks.

I laugh slightly as tears come to my eyes. "Let me get my bags out of the trunk first, then we can talk."

"Forget about that," she says. "We can get the bags later. Spill."

"I think he's been cheating on me."

"Oh no, Amelia. I'm so sorry," she says as she pulls me back into a hug. We stand there for several minutes before she speaks. "Come inside," she says, gesturing to the front door.

I follow her into the small house. Marigold never got married by choice, so she lives alone. The place is impeccable. There are no toys scattered around the living room or piles of laundry on the couch. Everything is right where it's supposed to be.

"Sit down," she says. "I'll make us some tea."

As she makes us tea, I think about how different our lives have turned out. She's been able to basically do whatever she wants without the responsibility of a husband and kids. Just last summer, she spent a month in Greece. Every time she'd post a picture on social media, I felt a pang of jealousy.

Sometimes, I wish I were strong enough to be alone. I've considered walking away from Garret many times and with the prenup, I'd be more than okay financially, but the idea of reentering the dating scene causes waves of panic and fear to rush through me. I just can't do it. What am I going to do?

Marigold brings two steaming cups of tea and hands me one. She sits across from me on a leather armchair, setting her tea down on the side table next to it. "Tell me more about what happened," she says. It's not really a request, but a command.

My voice trembles. "I found a note in his suitcase from another woman. Her name is Kora."

"That's a stupid name," she says.

I surprise myself with a laugh. "I don't know anything else," I tell her. "He's been going on these week-long business trips for months now and I just thought he was expanding his company, setting up a future for us. I'm so stupid. I should have known better."

She shakes her head. "No. I like that about you. You think the best of people."

"Well, I can't unsee that note," I reply. "There's no more thinking the best of Garret."

"What did he say when you asked him about it?" She asks.

I shake my head silently, ashamed.

"You didn't tell him?" She asks, not able to hide the

surprised look on her face. "Please tell me you're going to confront him."

"I don't know. I'm scared. I don't know that I really want to know the truth."

"You can't fight something if you don't know what you're up against," she says.

"But what if he lies to me? What if he gaslights me and tells me that it's not what I think it is? If I tell him that I know, then he'll just hide his tracks even better."

"True," she says, contemplating. "Well, in that case, we need to come up with a plan."

WE SPEND the entire weekend planning and devising how to find out more information. When I leave, I'm confident in the plan we've created and ready to implement it, but as I drive home, doubts trickle in. What if he catches me? What if I go through all this trouble and I don't find anything? A large sense of unease settles in the pit of my stomach. I don't know if I have what it takes to follow through with this.

I walk into the front door of our house. Garret is watching TV in the living room. Just the sight of him now makes me sick. How could he do this to me? I've given him everything he ever wanted. Or I've tried, at least.

I WAIT until Garret's asleep to implement the plan. He's snoring loudly when I quietly get out of bed and tiptoe to his nightstand. I slowly grab his phone, careful not to make any noise. My fingers are trembling and sweating. What if he wakes up and sees what I'm doing? I have to take that chance. If he does, I'll just tell him my phone died and I need to check the time. I take a deep breath and hold the phone up to his face. The light from the phone shines just brightly enough for it to unlock.

Garret stops snoring and starts moving around. Shoot. He's gonna catch me. I turn the phone back towards me to hide the light and stand as still as I can. Garret mumbles in his sleep, rolls over and begins to snore again. Relief floods my body.

I quietly sneak out of the room into the bathroom. I shut the door behind me and lock it. Sitting on the edge of the tub, I click on the texting app and look through his messages. I find nothing, only messages from me, his employees, his stupid group of sales buddies and what I assume are his clients.

Marigold's words echo in my mind. *Download a tracking app on his phone. That's the only way you're going to know what he's really up to.* I take a deep breath and find the app store, searching for a location-tracking app. I find one that mimics itself as a notepad app, quickly install it and then hide it in one of his folders.

As soon as I'm done, I quietly exit the bathroom, put the phone back on his nightstand and crawl back into my side of the bed. My heart continues to race for what feels like hours and I barely sleep a wink the rest of the night. I can't believe I did it. I have never invaded his privacy before, but anxiety and desperation have driven me over the edge. I convince myself that it's okay because I'm just looking for information. If he's telling the truth, I'll delete the app and forget about it, but if he isn't. . . I can't even process that thought.

THE NEXT MORNING, Garret packs his suitcase for what he tells me is a conference in New York. I watch him from my side of the bed as he packs. "Where are you staying this time?" I ask.

"Some hotel in downtown New York City. I don't even remember the name," he says nonchalantly. "My assistant set it up."

"Okay," I say, trying to mask my suspicion. "Have a safe flight."

He closes the suitcase and walks over to my side of the bed, planting a quick kiss on the top of my head. "See you Friday," he says.

I nod, afraid to even speak for fear that tears will unexpectedly fall out of my eyes.

As soon as he walks out the door, I grab my phone and download the same app I had installed onto his. I log in with the details I had created the night before and stare at the phone as I watch the little beacon head towards the airport. I watch it for over an hour, until it eventually disappears. He must be in the air. I force myself to close my phone.

Hours go by and anxiety is eating at me. Around dinner time, I give myself permission to check the app. I climb back down the stairs to where my phone is plugged into the kitchen outlet to face the truth.

I sit down at the table with a glass of wine and open the app. It takes a moment to load, but as soon as it does, my heart stops. Garret is not in New York. He is in L.A.

50

AMELIA (PAST)

The entire week that Garret is gone, the thoughts in my mind bounce all around. Sometimes I convince myself that he made a mistake about the location of the conference. Maybe he thought that it was in New York, but it was actually in Los Angeles. But then why didn't he text me and tell me as soon as he found out? These thoughts usually lead to me railing and screaming at him silently in my head. I then spend the next few hours slamming cupboards and banging around pots and pans.

Most of the days, I find myself somehow halfway in between complete trust in my husband's innocence and rage. Maybe this is just a one-time thing. Maybe it's not something that's been going on for months. By the time Thursday comes, I feel a bit unstable from the whirlwind of emotions. I gotta get myself under control.

I sit with a glass of wine on Thursday afternoon and force myself to figure out what to do. Does it matter to me if Garret is having an affair? Would that change my ultimate goal? I'm not sure if it really matters either way.

The truth is I don't want a divorce. I just want my

husband back. I know that I've changed. . . a lot. Maybe it's my fault he's not interested in me anymore.

When I was with my sister, she tried to convince me that it was insane for me to think that. I remember it vividly. "People don't get a free pass to cheat on their spouses just because they don't look the same way they did when they first met," she'd said. Her words resonate with me even now.

I would never cheat on him even if the tables were turned and he was the one who stopped taking care of himself. However, I know what I look like. I'm not the same woman I once was. Can I really blame him? Maybe I just need to try harder and seduce him in some way to remind him of the woman I used to be.

Then it hits me. I can do it tomorrow. Garret's coming home from his trip and I'm going to pull out all the stops.

EARLY THE NEXT AFTERNOON, I spend a few hours doing my hair, nails and makeup. I look through my closet and find a black lacy negligee that Garret bought for me once. I pull it over my head and wince as I struggle to put it on. It's a little tight, but it fits.

I look at myself in the mirror and smile. I look good. Almost like a different person than the one I saw this morning staring back at me. A wave of sadness washes over me. Why don't I do this kind of stuff anymore? It's not that I don't care about Garret. I'm just always so tired and the last thing I want to do is take care of myself. I need to be better about this; maybe Garret would stay home if I was.

At seven o'clock, I pull the dinner out of the oven: prime rib, baked potatoes and asparagus. All the things I know Garret likes. I even bought a chocolate cake earlier from our favorite bakery. I set everything on the table neatly, pour two glasses of wine and then light three candles in the middle of the table to give the room ambiance.

Fifteen minutes later, a car pulls up to the front of our house. I watch through the window as Garret walks towards the front door. This is it. This is my chance. I rush to the door, pause and take a deep breath. I smooth out my negligee and put on a smile before opening the door to greet him. I strike the most seductive pose I can manage in the doorframe and wait for him to look up and see me.

When he does, he looks confused.

"Surprise," I say as seductively as I can, trying to sound enticing.

He stops in his tracks, staring at me expressionless. "What is all this?" He asks, almost sounding annoyed.

"I made you a little something so we could have a romantic evening together," I reply.

He loosens his tie and unbuttons the top button of his shirt. "I don't know, Amelia. I'm tired. It's been a long week," he says.

He hasn't seen me in five days and he can't even pretend?

I try to stop it, but disappointment washes all over my face. I back away from the door and let him in.

He puts his stuff down by the stairs and turns to look at me. "Okay, fine. Just give me a few minutes to freshen up," he says.

Hope alights inside of me. This is it. This is my chance to win back my husband. I lock the front door and rush back into the kitchen. I throw each plate in the microwave for a couple of minutes to heat it back up, then sit patiently at the table, sipping my wine and waiting for him to come down.

By the time he does, I've nearly fallen asleep with my head resting on my hand. I perk myself up though, as soon as I hear his feet coming down the stairs.

He walks into the dining room wearing comfortable clothing, his hair touseled. He clearly didn't put any effort into his appearance. I can't help but feel disappointed.

"Babe, did you make that?" He asks, surprised.

I nod. "I know I'm not the greatest cook, but this seems to have turned out okay," I say.

"This looks amazing," he says genuinely.

He pulls out his chair and sits, eager to eat. His mood seems better, like all he needed was a few minutes to wipe off the stress of travel. I think he's warming up to me. We have surface-level conversations over dinner, mainly about his clients and the work he's doing.

"How was your conference?" I ask between bites.

"Huh?" He asks, looking up at me, confused at first. A moment later, realization dawns on his face. "Oh yeah, the conference. It was great. I learned a lot," he replies.

"What's New York like at this time of the year?" I ask.

"Cold," he says, laughing. "I should have brought a heavier coat. It's a good thing I was able to take a taxi everywhere because walking would have killed me."

I stare at him in disbelief. I'm amazed at the ease with which he lies directly to my face. It makes me question everything that he has said to me over the last few months. It's obvious lying has become a way of life for him, at least when it comes to me.

I wish that there was nothing that he felt like he had to hide from me. If he wasn't cheating on me, there would be no reason for him to lie. I just need him to make the right choice and come back home.

I refocus on making this one of the best nights of our lives. I hope everything I've done for this moment is worth it and that he realizes what he's going to lose if he follows through with his plans with Kora.

As soon as we're done, instead of clearing the dishes, I walk to the counter and give him the most seductive pose I possibly can.

To my surprise, he stands and kisses me. This is what I've been waiting for. I kiss him back with a passion that I thought was dormant. I should have done this a long time ago. I thought that I had lost touch with him, but his reaction to me right now tells me everything. I know what he wants. I know his heart. I am his wife.

I WAKE up the next morning feeling happy and content. I roll over to smile at Garret, only to find his side of the bed empty. "Garret?" I call. There's no answer. I turn back to my nightstand and grab my cell phone.

There's a message from Garret. *Sorry to leave without letting you know. You were sleeping so peacefully, I didn't want to wake you. I had to catch an early morning flight to Texas. There's some urgent business I have to attend to with one of my clients. I'm so sorry, babe. I know how much we were looking forward to spending the weekend together.*

My heart sinks as I look at the time. It's ten o'clock in the morning. I haven't slept this late in almost a decade. Probably more than a decade, to be honest. I wonder what time Garret left. It could have been hours ago and I would have never known. I pull up the tracking app on my phone and hold my breath as I wait for it to load. As soon as it does, I let out a sigh. Garret is not in Texas. He went back to L.A.

51

AMELIA (PAST)

My mind and my heart are in a panic. He's never left on the weekend before. I thought we had a good night. Why would he leave so suddenly?

I feel almost manic as I throw a change of clothes into a black bag. I get online and buy an overpriced last-minute ticket to L.A. A wave of guilt washes over me, but if I don't find out the truth about Garret, I'm going to make up something in my mind that is way worse than the actual truth.

I push my fears aside and focus on finding Garret. I will have nothing if my marriage doesn't work out. This has to be a priority.

I call a rideshare to take me to the airport; I'm in no position to drive.

During the flight, I down several tiny bottles of alcohol, hoping that they'll numb this raging panic that's in my chest and coursing through my veins. I just have to know who this woman is that Garret has been spending all his time with. Is she the same age as me? Younger than me? Does she have kids? The questions come in a barrage and I can't get them to stop, let alone answer all of them.

. . .

THE PLANE LANDS and I call a rideshare using the address I got from Garret's location as the destination. The driver navigates towards him and this mystery woman during the middle of rush hour traffic. It takes over an hour to get there, even though the address looks to be only thirteen miles from the airport.

Eventually, the driver pulls up to the apartment building and I hesitate. I don't know if I can do this.

I stare at the nondescript and rundown building where she lives for several minutes before working up the courage to get out of the car. I stand, frozen in my spot, uncertain of what to do next. Do I confront her, or do I stay out here and just watch for her? All I know is that I have to do something. The woman who lives here is the woman my husband has fallen for, the one he is planning on leaving me for. I won't go down without a fight.

Suddenly, I spot a couple walking down the sidewalk hand in hand and I gasp. Is that them? I glance around and find a large oak tree across the street from an apartment building. I rush behind the oak tree and take several deep breaths, hoping to calm my anxiety. I peek around the tree and watch them as they walk down the sidewalk. I'm too far away to get a good enough look. It looks like it could be Garret, but I'm not quite sure.

Out of nowhere, the man bursts out laughing. The sound of his voice makes my blood run cold. "That's Garret," I whisper. I would know that laugh anywhere. Just the sight of him with another woman constricts my lungs and I can hardly breathe.

I stare at them from behind the tree, desperately hoping they don't see me. They turn and walk up to the front door of the apartment building across the street. I watch as she unlocks the gate to the courtyard and they walk inside.

I leave my hiding spot and move to the edge of the street, hoping to catch a better glimpse of which apartment they enter. I can see the doors from here, but not any of the numbers. I consider crossing the street to get a better look, but I can't. I am rooted to this spot, unable to move or breathe.

I watch as they head up the stairs and enter the first apartment door on the left. A few seconds later, the light in the second-story window facing the street turns on and I see Garret clearly as he walks towards the window. The sound of their laughter drifts to the street. He sounds so happy. I can't remember the last time he laughed like that with me.

Who is this girl that has stolen his heart? Why her? What does she have that I don't have other than being young and pretty? Is she smarter than me? Or funnier than me? What is it about her that Garret is willing to do things for her that he wouldn't even consider doing for me? Those questions ruminate in my mind as I contemplate my next move.

52

AMELIA (PAST)

How am I going to learn more about her if I don't even know her name? I glance up and down the street, hoping to find inspiration, but I find nothing. I can't just stand here. What if they come back out of the apartment and see me?

I walk down the street and find a small park. I sit on a bench and put my head in my hands. What am I doing here? I didn't fly all the way here just to see where this girl lives. I need more information. If I go back now, this whole trip would have been for nothing.

I sit on the bench for the next hour and watch as people walk by, hoping that something will just come to me. I don't have all the time in the world. I have to get back before Garret, so whatever I do, it has to happen now.

Suddenly, a postal service worker walks by me, carrying a bag of mail. That's it. If I could somehow get her mail, I could figure out her name.

I watch the worker as they make their way down the street and then my heart sinks as I watch her unlock a large box and start filling it with mail. All of the mailboxes are locked. How am I going to get in there? Then it hits me: I'm going to have to break in, but how?

I spend the next thirty minutes searching the internet for ways to break into a locked mailbox. There's a surprisingly large amount of information out there if you look hard enough. I pick the method that seems the simplest and requires the least amount of tools. All I need is a screwdriver, one of those flat kinds.

I walk a few blocks, find a grocery store and grab one from their tiny tool department. I purchase it with cash and slip it into my purse. The sun is starting to go down, but I want to wait until it is fully dark outside before I make a move.

I walk back toward the apartment building and approach the front gate. My heart is pounding in my ears. What if they come out that door and see me? I can't get caught now. I stare through the gate at the door that they entered, trying to make out the gold numbers on the door. The courtyard is getting darker and darker by the moment and the numbers are impossible for me to read. I have to get inside.

A woman walks out of a unit on the first floor and walks towards the front door. This is my chance. I stand by the front door and pretend that I'm trying to figure out how to use the callbox. I press random buttons and pretend not to even notice her, but as soon as she walks out, I catch the gated door and slip inside.

The courtyard is small and unadorned. I sneak up the stairs, trying to be as quiet as possible. I even hold my breath for fear that it makes too much noise. I slow down as I approach the apartment.

There is a window that faces the courtyard and I slowly peek inside through a crack in the curtains. It allows me to see into the living room and all the way to the kitchen of the small apartment. Garret and this woman are standing in the kitchen making dinner together. Garret has a smile on his face that I haven't seen in years. They're laughing, drinking wine and working side by side. He's living an entirely different life with this woman, one that I am not even privy to. The sight of it breaks me in a way that I can't describe, but strengthens my resolve to find out who she is.

I sneak over to the door and in the dim light of the courtyard, I can finally read the number *203*.

I quickly walk out of the building and across the street. Now, all I have to do is wait until everyone is asleep.

I find a small diner where I can sit and wait without being noticed. I'm not hungry. My stomach is tied in knots about what I'm about to do. I'm pretty sure it's a felony to break into a mailbox, but by this point, I don't care. I can't leave here empty-handed.

I sit at the diner for several hours, waiting for the middle of the night to come. During that time, I drink at least five cups of coffee. My whole body feels jittery as I pay the bill and walk out of the diner. This is it. This is my chance.

I walk towards the apartment slowly, glancing around me as I go. I see not a single soul the entire way. The street is quiet and dark.

I get to the mailbox and turn the flashlight on my phone to illuminate the back of it. I find a gold medallion-looking keyhole on the back. It's on the very edge of the mailbox. As I shine my light at it, I can see the latch inserted into the side of the mailbox. From what I read, if I insert my screwdriver and push down as hard as I can, I can manually force the latch to unlock.

I insert the screwdriver into the crack and start pushing. The lock doesn't even budge. I push so hard that the wrench slips, making a loud grating sound along the edge of the metal. I stop and hold my breath, hoping that nobody heard that noise. I clutch the screwdriver at my side and glance around. A light turns on in one of the units and I quickly duck down and cover up the light coming from my phone. I sit as still as possible for several minutes, hoping and praying that no one can see me in the dark.

After a few minutes, the light turns back off. I release the breath I'm holding and force my heart to calm its rapid beating. I have to try again. This time, I try from the bottom up, pushing up as hard as I can. After a few seconds, the latch pops and the door opens.

I'm flooded with relief. I did it. I quickly look through the numbers on the mail slots hoping to find *203* quickly so I can get out of here. Within thirty seconds, I find it. Inside is a single piece of mail. I touch it and slowly pull it out of the hole and read the name — *Kora Mendez*. I hope it's not so generic that I can't find her on social media. At least now I've seen her; that should help. Even though I didn't get a very good look, I think it was enough.

I quickly pop the letter back into the mailbox and close the back door shut. I use my screwdriver to relatch it. I'm able to turn it just enough so that it stays closed. Maybe no one will even notice, or at least by the time they do, hopefully, I'll be long gone.

I check my watch, it's two am. I panic. I have to get back to the airport and find a flight home. I call a rideshare and on my way to the airport, I look up Kora Mendez on my phone. It doesn't take me long to find her. I'm immediately disappointed when I see that her page is completely private. I'm going to have to become friends with her to find out more about her.

The only things I'm able to see on her page are posts by

someone who made them public, maybe by accident. The first one is a picture of a cat playing in the water. *Isn't he cute?* It reads just above the photo. There's another picture of a cat climbing a tree with the caption, *I hope they were able to get this little baby down.* I look at the name of the poster. Marissa Mendez. I wonder if that's her mom.

I click on the post and I'm taken to a page of a woman who looks to be in her early sixties. Her profile picture shows her holding a light gray cat next to her face and the banner on her page shows several cats lying around a park. This lady is obsessed with cats.

Then it hits me, this is the way into Kora's life. Taking a deep breath, I craft a new identity. A cat lover named Cathy Whitman, complete with photos of cats I've found online and memes about being a cat mom. It seems harmless enough. I send Marissa a friend request and to my surprise, she accepts it almost immediately.

Scrolling through Marissa's posts, it's clear she's incredibly proud of Kora. There are photos of Kora singing at various venues, graduating from college and taking vacations. The captions are all glowing, full of motherly pride. *My talented daughter! So proud of her recent gig at The Viper Room!* Reads one. *Kora, looking radiant as ever in Malibu,* reads another.

It stings, seeing all these photos, but it also gives me a timeline, a sense of who she is and perhaps more importantly, how she and Garret might have met. The more I dig, the more I piece together. Kora's a singer, making her way up in the L.A. scene. She's talented and she's driven.

Over the next several days, I am active on my page. I start requesting anyone that Marissa interacts with and commenting on all of her cat photos. She doesn't immediately reply to any of the comments at first, but one day, she posts a picture of a cat jumping from one roof to another. I immediately comment on the post. *I sure hope that poor kitty made it.*

Marissa almost immediately replies. *I can't believe how often the little babies risk their lives.* From there, we started a conversation on the post and we eventually moved it to a private message. We talked for hours, first about cats, but then about our jobs and where we live. I had fun with it, making everything up as I went. After several hours, it felt like Marissa and Cathy were best friends.

Over the next several weeks, Marissa and I talk off and on, becoming even closer. I keep a notebook with me at all times to make sure I keep my story straight.

I mentioned you to my daughter., she says late one afternoon. *She thinks I'm crazy for talking to you so much. I showed her your page and she doesn't even think you're a real person.*

LOL, I respond, trying to keep my tone light when inside, I am filled with anxiety and dread. What if all this work I've been doing getting to know Marissa is for nothing?

I dismissed her immediately. Of course, you're real. You are an amazing person, Marissa says. *She did ask me a question that I wasn't sure how to answer. How come you don't have a profile picture of yourself?*

I sigh. I can handle this. *I'm just a little embarrassed about how I look. I don't feel comfortable having it out there on the internet.*

Makes sense, Marissa says. *Well, I told my daughter she should just be friends with you so she can see how real of a person you actually are.*

This is it. This is my moment. I head over to Kora's page and hit the friend request button. Within seconds, I receive notification that my request has been accepted. My heart soars as I realize what I've done. I'm in.

53

AMELIA (PAST)

What I find on Kora's social media page makes my heart drop. Interspersed with posts about the gigs that she's doing are pictures of Kora and Garret at all different locations across L.A. They look like tourists exploring the city and Garret looks happier than I think I've ever seen him, but everything posted here is curated and planned. I need to know what things are really like between them and I'm never going to figure that out by stalking this page. There has to be another way.

I perform another deep dive on the internet and I find more than just websites about breaking into mailboxes. There's a whole world of information out there on how to do all sorts of illegal things. I don't want to do anything crazy; I just need to know what's going on between the two of them. All I want is to somehow hear the conversations Garret has with her.

I know he probably talks to her while he's home on the weekends, but where? Then it hits me. Garret's home office has always been his private sanctuary, the one place in our house he doesn't want me to interfere with. He'll often go in there, shut the door and be in there for hours. He tells me it's because he's got tons of work to do, but maybe there's more to it than that.

I buy a listening device off the internet that syncs to my phone. It will record any conversation that occurs within ten feet of it.

THE DEVICE COMES a week later in a nondescript package. Garret is gone, so now is as good of a time as any to install it.

I walk into his office. It's immaculately clean. The weight of the tiny listening device feels immense in my hand. I stand rooted to the floor in the middle of the room. This feels like a last-ditch attempt to claw back some semblance of control in a situation that feels increasingly out of my grasp. A part of me feels guilty for listening in on his conversations, but I quickly shove that aside. I need to know.

I take a deep breath. I slide the device under his desk, careful to position it near where he usually sits. I exit the room quickly, my heart pounding. Back in our bedroom, I connect the device to my phone through the app provided by the company. I walk back into the room and say a few quick words, immediately seeing a recording pop up on my screen. It works.

I plug in the headphones and open the corresponding app on my phone. Every rustle, every shift of the chair, sounds crystal clear. I almost feel like I'm still in the room.

When Garret comes home the next weekend, it's all I can do to not check the app every minute of every day he's here. However, I control myself and wait until he leaves on Monday to listen.

The first few weekends, the recordings consist of sales calls to clients and a phone call to his mother. He must not talk to Kora often on the phone; they probably mostly text. I consider taking his phone again and searching through it, but then I remember that he deleted all the messages from her. It would be pointless.

Four weeks after installing the device, I finally hit the jackpot. I fast-forward through the beginning of the conversation, where they spend several minutes telling each other how much they love each other. After the first five minutes, I press play.

"Baby, you know I love you," Garret says. Since I can only hear Garret's end of the conversation, I have to infer what she's saying on the other end. After several seconds of silence, he continues. "I promise I'm going to end things with Amelia soon so we can be a family together."

My heart stops. The note she wrote was true. He's telling her that he's going to leave me.

"I swear," he insists emphatically. "I can't do this anymore. Every time I'm here with her, I miss you like crazy."

The room begins to spin. His words hit me like a punch to the gut, taking the breath from my lungs. Tears blur my vision, but I force myself to continue listening to hear every painful word. After all, this is what I wanted — the truth, finally.

The conversation ends and I'm left with deafening silence. The reality of it all crashes down on me. The man that I love, the man that I built my life with, is going to leave me.

I sit on the edge of the bed, numb. How do I stop this? How do I make him realize he's making a huge mistake, that I'm his family and that the grass is not greener on the other side?

54

AMELIA (PAST)

The amber glow of the evening sun streaks through the curtains as I sit in our bedroom, earphones plugged in, ready to listen to Garret's conversations. I've made a ritual of it over the last few weeks; every day when he's home after he disappears into his home office, I tune in.

Each time breaks me like I'm submitting myself to some kind of medieval torture, but I can't stop. I don't know; maybe I hope things will sour between him and Kora and he'll realize that he loves me and wants to end things with her, but it never happens. Instead, their conversations are filled with plans for the upcoming week and how much they love each other; it makes me sick.

I keep hoping that I'll hear something, anything, that I can use to win him back, but each conversation only serves to make me feel even more and more hopeless.

Tonight, the conversation I overhear chills me to the bone. It doesn't start out the same as it usually does. Garret is immediately on edge.

"Look, Kora," Garret's voice sounds tense. "We need to

do something about Amelia. If we go through with a divorce, she'll take half of everything. I can't let that happen."

My breath catches in my throat. This isn't just him promising to leave me anymore. I wish I could hear what's being said on the other end of the line. The silence as Garret waits to respond puts me on pins and needles.

"I hear what you're saying, Kora," he says, "but we have to get rid of her for good." The air in the room feels cold. I take the blanket from the bed and wrap it around me in an attempt to take away the bitter cold I feel in my bones, but the weight of his words bears down on me. Are they going to kill me?

Garret continues. "I know you didn't sign up for this, but it's the only way. If you love me, you'll support me in this. Please, just trust me."

My mind races in the silence. What are they going to do? How is Garret going to get rid of me? Is he even capable of it? If you had asked me months ago, I would have vehemently said you were crazy, but now, I'm uncertain. The man I thought I was married to would have never done any of this.

He continues again. "I want us to be a family. No distractions, no outside influences. That's not going to happen if Amelia and I just get divorced. There's no other way."

My heart sinks. He's going to kill me. There's no way he could do it himself; he's too much of a coward. Is he going to hire a hitman? My fears are confirmed by his next words.

"Let me talk to someone, figure out what it would take. I don't want to do this, Kora, but I have to do it for us. Please, just trust me."

There's more silence. Garret's voice is pleading. "No, don't do that, Kora. Please."

I hear Garret set the phone down on the desk. I pull the headphones from my ears, my fingers trembling. What am I going to do?

Over the next hour, I question myself, wondering if I made the entire thing up. Maybe I misunderstood. Doubts plague my mind. I feel like maybe I'm going crazy.

I make spaghetti and meatballs for dinner, one of Garret's favorites. Garret is supposed to come out of his office and join me, but there's no telling if he actually will. He surprises me when he shows up on time for dinner, but he's in a sour mood. Usually, he's happy when he sits at the table, on a high from his conversation with Kora, but today is different.

He walks down the stairs, immediately goes to the liquor cabinet and pours himself a glass of whiskey.

"What's wrong?" I ask hesitantly. When he gets like this, I usually try to avoid him, but today, I just can't. I need to know. Not that I think he's going to tell me about this plan to kill me, but maybe he'll accidentally give me some information that sheds some more light on the situation.

"Nothing," he says curtly. "Just a hard day. I need some time to myself."

He makes himself a plate of food and walks straight back to his office.

Something must have happened with Kora. I can feel it. I quickly rush to our bedroom and take out my computer. I log into my social media and navigate to Kora's page like I've done a million times in the past. It looks different. All the pictures of Garret have been removed. I click on her friends list and Garret is no longer listed as one of her friends. Hope springs up, but is quickly dashed as I remember Garret's mood. He doesn't want this.

I wonder if she is distancing herself from him because he's taking too long to do what he promised he would do. They must have been in on this together and Garret has been dragging his feet. I'm obviously still alive and she's tired of waiting. Fear grips me. This is only going to push Garret to make the necessary moves to get her back. My life is on the line. He's going to end me so that he can be with her. I can feel it in my bones.

I have to do something. If Garret is planning to hurt me, I have to be one step ahead, or my life is going to be over. This is no longer about winning Garret back. This is about stopping him from ending my life. My survival instincts kick in as a plan begins to form in the back of my mind.

55

AMELIA (PRESENT)

"Help, please," I scream. My voice is hoarse. I've been pounding on the closed door and screaming for what feels like hours, but no help has come. I'm never gonna get out of here. Desperation seizes me and I pound one last time on the door, yelling at the top of my lungs and then slide to the ground. I bring my knees to my chest and hug them tightly.

I can't believe Miles locked me in a closet just because I found out he knew Kora. He knows how guilty it makes him look and he couldn't bear the idea of everyone else interrogating him just like they've been interrogating Garret. He's a coward.

At least Garret acknowledges his relationship with Kora. I mean, it would have been a little hard to deny it after the way he looked at her last night at dinner. Everyone saw it. Actually, it would have been impossible to deny. Maybe Garret and Miles aren't that much different. Garret had no choice and Miles threw me in here to keep me quiet so he wouldn't be forced to come clean.

I can't believe Garret didn't let me out. I swear he saw

me. He stared right at me and then walked the other way. What kind of a person does that to their wife? I've done nothing to deserve that. All I've done is help him since we've been here.

What if nobody finds me in here until it's too late? I have no food and no water. How long can a person go without water? Three days? I shiver from the cold that seeps through the closet's walls and into my bones. It dawns on me. I don't even have to worry about dying from starvation or dehydration. The cold is going to get me first.

I begin to pace the tiny room, trying to keep my temperature up. I don't know how much longer I have. If I stop moving for even a few seconds, my body starts to shake. I have to do more to keep my body heat up. I start jogging in place. My temperature slowly rises, but I can't do this forever. I have to get out. I can't die in here.

I stare at the door. Maybe I can run into it and break it. I step to the back wall and run as hard as possible into the door, jamming my right shoulder into the hard metal. It doesn't even budge. "This isn't going to work," I mutter, rubbing my shoulder. The door is going to break me before I break it.

I look around the room, hoping to find anything that can help. My eyes land on a toolbox. Maybe there is something in there that I can use.

I grab the box, set it on the floor and open it. Inside, I find several tools. I look at the door. How can I use these tools to get myself out? I scour the surface of the door and run my hands over it. The metal is cool to the touch. Aside from the small window at the top, the solid mass has no obvious cracks or weaknesses.

I glance around the edges and notice the hinges that connect the door to the frame. What if I could get those apart somehow? I touch one and examine it. It looks like there's some kind of metal pin inserted in the top to hold the hinges together. Maybe I can get that pin out, but how?

I rifle through the toolbox once more. I come upon a flat-head screwdriver. "I can use this," I whisper. I grab it and walk towards the door. If I push hard enough, I can use this to take the pin out of the hinge. I set the head of the screwdriver just under the lip of the pin and push as hard as I can. The pin doesn't budge. "Come on," I yell. I need to hit it harder, or it will never come out.

I grab the hammer out of the toolbox. I'll use this to create more force. Maybe it will be enough to get the pin to budge. I pound on the handle of the screwdriver with the hammer. It's hard work. The hammer slips several times and I whack myself in the hand.

The fourth time the hammer slips, it hits my thumb. "Dang it," I yell. The pain is immediate and it hurts so bad that I'm convinced it is broken. I can't move it. Every time I try, pain rips through my thumb and radiates up my arm. If it's broken, I am never getting out of here. I can't panic. I take several deep breaths, forcing myself to calm down and try to move my finger again. It still doesn't move, but the pain is not as severe.

I sit on the ground, defeated. I'm going to die in here. I don't deserve this. After ten minutes of feeling sorry for myself, I try to move my thumb again. This time, I can move it slightly and relief floods my body. At least it's not broken.

"Help," I yell again before resuming my assault on the door hinges. I don't actually believe anyone is going to hear me, but I have to at least try.

More time goes by, I give up yelling and resume removing the door pin. I swing at the screwdriver again, but

I am a little more cautious this time. If I hit my finger one more time, I might actually break it and then I'm screwed.

I want to give up several times, but I keep going because I notice small changes in the position of the pin each time I hit it. It takes a long time, but eventually, one of the pins pops out of the door. I did it. Pride surges through me. I guess I'm stronger than I ever realized.

I stare back at the door — only two more to go. Several minutes later, the other two pins are out and I have no new bruises on my hands, but the door doesn't fall. I don't know what I expected to happen, but I wasn't expecting it to remain standing.

I stare at it for several minutes, but nothing happens. Why didn't it fall? I realize there's still a lock on the other side of the door, keeping it attached to the door frame. I shove the door and it moves slightly. Maybe if I run into it this time with some speed behind me, something will break.

I step again to the back of the room and then run as fast as I can to the door. Pain erupts in my already bruised shoulder, but the door budges slightly and a splintering sound comes from the frame near the handle. Ignoring the pain, I back up again and run straight at the door, slamming all of my weight into it. Again, it budges only slightly, but this time, I see the beginnings of cracks in the frame around the lock. It's working.

I spend the next few minutes running as hard as I can into the door before the lock finally splinters and the door falls to the ground. I did it. I can't believe I got out of here. I shake my head in amazement.

I look at my hands. They're bleeding in several places and bruised from the hammer. Sharp pain erupts in my shoulder, but I don't care. I'm free. I charge out of the room and into the corridor. I have to find Garret.

56

MILES

I open the generator room door, fully expecting to see Amelia still trapped in the closet. I'm shocked when I see the door lying on the ground and the wood frame of the lock splintered all around it. How did she get out?

I quickly look around the room to ensure she's not in there. What if she comes back and finds me? What will she do to me? I have to find what I'm looking for and get out of there as quickly as possible.

In my haste, I forget to close the door behind me as I rush to the computer. I turn the computer on and begin looking through the files from the camera right outside of Kora's room. Each file holds twelve hours of video. I open the most recent file, rewind the film to yesterday afternoon and begin to watch every frame meticulously, hoping to find the truth.

For the most part, the videos are uneventful. The hallway is empty and there is nothing going on. Occasionally, an employee will walk through the screen as they head to their own rooms, but I am able to fast-forward through most of it.

After what feels like forever, I finally see Kora on the screen. I slow the video down and watch as she leaves the room, dressed in her evening gala attire for her performance. My heart stops. She looks so beautiful. I can't believe she's gone.

I fast-forward and watch as she comes back to her room after the performance. She opens the door and goes into her room. Moments later, I see another figure come down the hallway. It looks like Garret, but I can't quite tell because his back is to the camera. She opens the door and lets him inside. My heart drops. I fast-forward. Only a few minutes pass on the footage and it looks like she is kicking him out of her room. In the doorway, he grabs her elbow. She turns around and looks at him, clearly unhappy. She is unhappy, but she is alive. No, there must be more to the story.

I can't hear what they're saying, but it looks like they're yelling at each other. Kora is raising her hands in angry gestures. Garret is putting up both hands, trying to draw her close. He was with her last night after her performance; why did he lie if he was innocent?

His lie weighs on me as I watch Garret grab Kora and kiss her. She struggles against him, pushing on his chest, but he doesn't let go. Even from the grainy footage, I can feel the tension in Kora's body as she shoves violently against Garret's chest. The room feels cold around me as the truth of what I'm watching hits me.

A sound from behind me makes me jump. Turning, I see Garret, his face pale, eyes wide with horror as he watches the footage unfold on the screen. Our eyes lock and the air grows thick with tension.

"You got that on tape?" He asks, trembling.

"Yeah, I did," I say. "That thing between you and Kora wasn't just casual, was it?" I ask.

He steps closer to me and I take a step back away from him. If he gets too close, I don't know what will happen. I need to keep my distance.

"It's not what it looks like," he says. "I mean, yeah. It wasn't just casual. I loved her, but I didn't hurt her."

I chuckle, the bitterness evident in my tone. "It looks to me like you were trying to force her to do something against her will. Maybe it's not evidence of you actually killing her, but it's definitely evidence of motive."

"No," he yells as he lunges at me without warning. His arms reach for me and I'm caught off guard. I stumble back and extend my arms towards him, trying to fend him off.

He grabs me and takes me to the ground. Our bodies are intertwined as we grapple and bump into the generator. The lights flicker for a few seconds and turn back on. Our movements are desperate and chaotic. We continue to roll around, knocking over two chairs in the process. They clatter to the ground loudly, but we don't stop.

He rolls me over and jumps on top of me, gaining the upper hand. He holds down both of my arms with his hands and places his knees on my thighs. "I can't let you show anyone that footage. I can't go to jail for something I didn't do," he says desperately.

"It's pretty evident to me you did something."

"No, I didn't, I swear!" he says, panicking.

Garret raises one of his fists and just as he's about to punch me in the side of the head, the door to the room slams all the way open. Garret stops himself and glances over at the door, distracted by what he sees.

I don't even bother to look. Instead, I take the opportunity to get Garret off balance. I shove him off of me and roll him onto his back. Gaining the upper hand, I get on top of him and put my knees on his arms, pinning him down. I pound him in the face as hard as I can. He killed Kora. He killed the love of my life. I can't let him get away.

57

AMELIA

The end of this corridor is dark and empty. If I didn't know any better, I would think this place had been abandoned. The only sounds are my footsteps in the hall.

"Where the heck are you, Garret?" I whisper. My voice echoes in the silence, causing the hairs on the back of my neck to rise. I have to get out of here.

I have checked nearly the entire abandoned wing of this resort and Garret is nowhere in sight. I've tried every door handle and looked inside every unlocked room. Nothing. Most of the rooms looked like they were being used for storage, but a few looked like they'd been occupied recently. Who would stay on this side of the building? I barely want to stay in the part that's renovated.

I open the doors to the last two rooms in this hallway. The first room is full of empty shelves. I shine the light around the room and find nothing but cobwebs. The second room looks like it's being used as a bedroom. There's a bed in one corner and a dresser with a mirror in the other.

I shine the light under the bed to make sure Garret is not

hiding there. As soon as I do, a beady pair of yellow eyes reflects brightly in the beam of my flashlight. I scream and jump back against the wall behind me. The noise terrifies the creature and it scampers from under the bed, brushing past my leg as it exits the room.

"What the heck was that?" I yell.

I shine my light down the hallway after the creature. Its dark brown fur and stumpy legs move quickly. Just before it turns the corner, I see the tell-tale white markings on its face — a raccoon. I breathe a sigh of relief as it disappears from sight.

I quickly close the bedroom door and pause for a second to determine my next move. I should head back to the generator room and look at the security cameras. Maybe I can find him quicker that way.

I walk back towards the generator room. As soon as I enter the corridor where the room is located, I hear yelling erupt through the closed door.

What in the world is going on? I pick up my pace and start jogging towards the room.

The moment I open the door, Garret looks at me. His jaw is clenched and there's fire in his eyes. I watch as Miles shoves him over, climbs on top of him and begins to pummel his face.

"Stop, Miles? What are you doing?" I ask, rushing towards him.

Miles continues to attack Garret in a blind rage, not even acknowledging my existence.

I wrap my arms around his waist and pull as hard as I can, trying to yank him off. I'm not quite strong enough to get him completely off, but I provide enough of a lift that Garret is able to shove him and scramble to his feet.

Miles slowly stands. Both men are panting, but their fight has been temporarily suspended.

"He attacked me," Miles says, pointing a finger at Garret.

"Over what?" I ask, even though I'm pretty sure I know the answer.

"He killed Kora," Miles replies, his voice growing louder with each word.

"No, I didn't," Garret says, defending himself. "I didn't do what he's accusing me of."

Miles's fists clench and unclench as if he's contemplating putting his hands on Garret again. Tears rush down his cheeks. "Yes, you did. I know it."

"How?" I ask, glancing between Garret and Miles.

Miles continues to glare at Garret, but points at the computer screen.

I look over and my heart stops — an image of Garret and Kora kissing is suspended on the screen. I move closer to get a better look. While the image is grainy, I can see that Kora has both of her hands on Garret's chest as if she's trying to push him away. I find the button to zoom in on the image and gasp as it becomes clearer. The expression on Kora's face is not one of love, but panic.

I look back at Garret. "I thought the two of you were in love. Why does she look like she's trying to run away from you?" I question.

"We are, I mean, we were in love," he sighs. "It's just complicated. I didn't want you to find out like this, Amelia. This is such a mess."

Miles lunges at Garret again. "You killed her," he screams.

This time, Garret is ready. He sticks out his leg and trips Miles as he runs toward him, sending him to the ground. He immediately jumps on top of Miles to return the earlier blows. They are locked in a fierce struggle, throwing punches and knocking over chairs and equipment.

"Stop it!" I yell, but they both completely ignore me.

Miles gains the upper hand again and punches Garret in the face. Garret covers his face with his arms to protect himself.

I have to stop this. As angry as I am at Garret right now, I can't let him die.

I watch them, unsure of what to do. Both men are much bigger and stronger than me and the fight this time is much more violent than it was when I first walked in. I can't just get in the middle without getting hurt myself.

Miles's back is turned to me. Maybe I can knock him off balance somehow. I run at him with full force, catching him off guard and knocking him to the ground.

Garret scrambles back on top and deals a blow right to Miles's temple.

Miles's arms drop immediately to the ground. He's out cold.

Garret slowly rises, his breath ragged. He looks at me with an admiration that I haven't seen in years. "You saved my life," he says, panting and shaking his head.

My hands tremble as I stare at Miles's body. "I think you killed him," I whisper, panic rising in my chest.

Garret shakes his head. "No, I don't think he's dead. He's probably just knocked out, but we shouldn't stick around here to find out."

He grabs my hands. "Amelia, I'm so sorry about all this, but I want to fix things between us. I want us to be together."

I can't process his words, as my mind is fixed on the unconscious man lying on the ground. My hands tremble as the realization of what we've done hits me. "It was self-defense. We had no choice," I whisper, my voice quivering.

"I was just defending you and you were just defending yourself."

Garret's grip on my hands tightens. "I know, Amelia. I know, but I don't think he's dead. I'm not sure how long we have before he wakes up."

I look at Garret and shake my head. "I just wanted us to be good. For our marriage to be good."

"And we will be," he says. "I promise." He wraps his arms around me in an attempt to comfort me. It doesn't work. I can't be comforted when my entire world feels like it is falling apart.

58

AMELIA

Garret continues to hold me in a strong embrace that I would have welcomed just yesterday, but now it feels suffocating.

It dawns on me. While what I did was clearly self-defense, what Garret did was more than that. He didn't have to hit him in the head. I push on Garret's chest, forcing him to let me go. "You killed him," I say, glaring at him in disgust. "All you had to do was deny his allegations and walk away, but you had to fight about it."

"I told you, he's not dead, Amelia. I didn't hit him hard enough to kill him."

I'm not convinced. His body lies there, unanimated. There's no movement in his chest. Nothing. I could put my hand next to his mouth to see if there's air escaping, but I'm too scared. What if he really is dead? How do we hide this from the police? I'm not going to jail over this.

I walk away from Garret and look around the room. My eyes land on the computer and the image of Garret forcing himself on Kora. "We have to get rid of the files on that computer," I whisper.

"Do you think you can do that?" Garret asks hopefully.

I look at him in disgust. "Lucky for you, we've been in the middle of a blizzard and there's been a power outage. If I go in and delete everything from the time the outage started, the police will have no reason to look into it further."

"Yes, yes, let's do that," Garret says eagerly.

I shake my head. "I thought you didn't kill Kora. Why are you so worried?"

"Yeah, of course I didn't, but I also don't want them to find out what happened to Miles. Wouldn't it be better if there was no evidence at all of any of it? They can't charge us for something they don't know we did."

"What you did," I whisper. "All I did is knock Miles off of you."

"Fine," he says exasperated. "What I did. Does it really matter? We were both here."

I stare at the screen with resolve. "Yes, less evidence would be better."

I walk over to the computer. The image of Garret and Kora remains frozen on the screen. It hasn't locked since Miles logged in. Anyone with access to this room could get to this stuff. I shake my head. I can't worry about that right now.

I navigate to the desktop, select all the files from the time the blizzard started and delete them.

"That's it?" Garret asks, "They're gone?"

I nod. He doesn't know any better.

"I don't deserve you," Garret says. "After everything I've put you through, you're still here for me, protecting me. Why?"

I turn to him. "Not everything is about you, Garret."

He looks away, clearly ashamed. "Of course," he whispers.

I shake my head. What did I ever see in him? He always made me feel like I was lesser than him because I never went back into tech, but now I see that I am the glue that holds everything together. Without my constant efforts, our relationship wouldn't exist. He's put me and so many others through so much pain. He doesn't care about anyone, but himself. He never loved me or Kora. It would almost be better if Garret died.

I close my eyes and contemplate the situation. I have to find a foolproof way to delete the files, but in the meantime is there anything else that needs to be addressed before we leave this room?

I stare at the generator and see the cord running from it to the computer. If it looks like there's power to the computer, then the police are going to know that someone tampered with the files.

I look up at Garret. "We need to reset this room to how it was before I routed power to the computer. It must look like it's not had power since the outage happened."

"Tell me what to do," he says.

We spend the next several minutes resetting everything to its original position. I unplug the cords, twisting them up and putting them in the corner of the room exactly as they were when I first came in. Garret picks up the chairs and puts them back. We can do nothing about the closet door, so we leave that alone.

When we finish, I walk over to the computer screen and try to turn it on. I'm encouraged by the lack of lights and the darkness emanating from the glass. "No power," I say. "It's off."

Garret sighs; his face, once filled with tension, relaxes slightly. "Thank you," he murmurs, relief evident in his tone.

I nod, but I barely listen. My mind is racing with all that has happened in the past two days. First Kora, now Miles. It is almost too much to handle.

59

AMELIA

The anger inside of me builds as I stare at this man who I once loved, but now makes me sick.

"What is it?" He asks hesitantly.

With the cameras off, I find a courage I didn't have before. "You think I'm a fool," I say quietly.

"What?" He asks, shocked. "No, not at all."

I take a step toward him. "You've been playing me for months, Garret, possibly even years. You relied on the fact that I believed everything you ever said to me. You took advantage of that and did whatever you wanted."

"I'm so sorry, Amelia. I never meant to hurt you."

He reaches out his hands to touch me and I bat them away. The thought of his touch makes me want to vomit.

"I thought you were trying to get rid of me," I say sarcastically. "But now you're so eager to touch me and love me. Which is it, Garret?"

"What are you talking about?" He asks quietly.

"Oh, I heard your conversations with Kora. All of the ones you made from the privacy of your office over the past several weeks."

A look of shock crosses his face. "How?"

"That's not important. What is important is what you said," I say, poking him in the shoulder with my finger. "You told Kora it would only be a few more weeks before I was gone. And now you're telling me you didn't mean that?"

He shakes his head. "I didn't, I swear. I was just telling her what she wanted to hear."

"Hmmm," I say, clearly unconvinced. "So what did you mean exactly when you said you'd get rid of me? It sounded to me like you were trying to kill me."

"Never," he says, his eyes wide. He steps away from me and puts his hands up in defense. "I just meant we were going to get a divorce... that I was going to leave you."

"I heard you, Garret," I say, my voice rising. "You clearly told her that divorce wouldn't be enough, that I was going to take everything from you."

He stammers, unable to come up with another lie.

"I'm not as foolish as you thought I was, am I?" I ask with a sinister smile.

"You have it all wrong," he says with fear in his eyes.

I shake my head in disgust. "For months now, you've been preying on my trust. You left me alone for days at a time and wouldn't even answer the phone. It's as if you don't even care that I exist."

"Don't say that," he says, hurt crossing his face.

"Oh, I'm not falling for that. Not anymore," I say as I slowly bend down and pick up the camera I had left next to the generator earlier. I grab it and hold it by the straps with both hands. "You know what I've learned, Garret, in just the last twenty-four hours?"

He shakes his head, slowly backing away from me. "What are you doing, Amelia? What's going on?"

"I've learned that I'm better than you. Every move you

make is so obvious. You make yourself look guilty from your stupidity."

"What are you talking about?"

"You really know nothing, do you? You thought you had it all figured out. You planned on me continuing to be in the dark, but I'm not anymore."

"I never thought that," he says, panic rising in his voice.

"You do know that me deleting that footage doesn't actually save you, right?"

"But it's gone. How can they pin something on me if there's no evidence."

"Do you really not know how anything works? Nothing is permanently deleted. If they wanted to, they could easily retrieve all of those videos. All it would take is a good computer technician."

His face is as white as snow as the implications of my words sink in.

Miles groans. I see him moving slightly on the ground in the corner of my eye.

Garret glances at him briefly.

I don't dare to look, not wanting to give Garret the upper hand. "You're so lucky. At least you won't have another murder pinned on you."

"I didn't kill Kora either. I swear," he says pleadingly.

"You left me locked in that room and look at what you did to Miles," I say. "You sure do look guilty."

Garret takes a breath. "Fine. The truth is that I had to kill her. She was going to destroy everything we built. It's the main reason I went along with this trip. When you told me about it, I knew that she was performing here. I didn't know how you found out about her and set it up, but I figured I'd take advantage before everything fell apart. I wanted to make it look like an accident. An overdose."

And just like that, the truth. Finally.

"So you did do it?" I ask.

"Does it matter now? She's gone."

His eyes are distant as he remembers his actions. Does he actually expect me to feel sorry for him? It's not Kora's fault that he pursued her. He is the one who should be dead. He doesn't notice as I clutch the camera tighter.

He continues. "I'm sorry. For everything."

"Don't worry. You won't go to prison." I know the truth now. As long as he is alive, I will be in danger because I know who he really is. This has to happen.

I swing the camera as hard as I can and it hits Garret in the temple with a sickening thud. He immediately falls backward onto a desk. I quickly swing the camera at him again. He tries to block it, but it is no use; the camera cracks against his temple and he falls to the ground. Blood pools in the crevice left by the lens and drips down the side of his face. I walk over to him and check his pulse, fully prepared to hit him again if necessary. There's nothing; he's dead.

I am doing what I should have done a long time ago. I am taking back control of my life.

I look around the room. I have to make it look like we fought and I had no choice, but to kill him. I look down at my clothes and rip them in several places, making myself look disheveled. I mess up my hair and wipe some of Garret's blood on my shirt. Thankfully, I'm still beat up from clawing my way out of the closet.

I turn on my phone and check my reflection with the camera. I look like I've been through war. Now, all I need to do is act like it.

I practice a look of devastation in my reflection on a blank computer monitor. Once I'm confident I've perfected it, I take a deep breath. It's not a lie; I was a distraught and devastated wife, but I am not a victim. Just one good performance and I can be free of him for good.

60

AMELIA

I tuck my phone into my back pocket and prepare myself for the role of a lifetime. I'm just about to exit the door when I glance at the computer. I still have something to do — the video footage.

I quickly plug the computer back in and wait anxiously for it to turn back on. Miles groans again from his position on the floor. I don't have much time.

As soon as the computer turns on, I navigate to the recycle bin and restore all the videos I had previously deleted. I want the evidence of Garret being in the room to stay, but there's a different video I have to remove.

I click through the files, looking for the one that I want. I find Garret entering Kora's room with a wine bottle in his hand. It's easy to miss, but it's definitely there. In the footage, it's only moments later that she kicks him out and they fight. Still, this is not what I'm looking for.

I finally find it. It's dark, but it's still clear enough to see the image of me knocking on Kora's door, her talking to me and letting me in. No one can know that I went in there. If they did, all of this would have been for nothing. I have to get rid of it.

I quickly delete the file, navigate to the recycle bin and delete it from there as well. That's probably not enough. There's a gap in the videos. A good detective will figure out that one is missing. They'll probably hire some forensic computer person to hunt down the file I deleted. I know enough to know that those things never go away for good.

As much as I want the evidence of Garret being with Kora to remain, it's too risky. I have to figure out a way to destroy the files and make them inaccessible. I need a magnet.

I look around the room for inspiration. I spot the key card device on the door to the room. There has to be a magnet in there, something that causes the door to lock and unlock with a keycard. If I can just get it out, maybe that will be enough to destroy the footage. But how?

Panic rises in me as Miles makes another groan. If he sees me doing this, all is lost. I look past him and spot the open door to the storage room. I used a screwdriver and a hammer to get myself out of that room; maybe I could use them to pry the device off the door.

I step gingerly over Miles and quietly head into the room that was, just a little while ago, my prison. I find the screwdriver and hammer lying on the floor right inside the door.

I take them over to the main door and use them to try to pry the key card panel off. It doesn't budge at first, but I don't quit. I dig the screwdriver into the top of the metal box covering the tech and hit it as hard as I can with the hammer. A small crack forms at the top of the device, filling me with hope. I can do this. I keep hammering as the device slowly separates from the door, little by little. I practically destroy it in the process, but I don't care.

Small beads of sweat form on my brow and I wipe them away with my arm. Just a few more hits. When it eventually comes off, it is cracked and many of the wires are severed, but the internal workings are still intact. I look inside and see something that looks like it could be a magnet.

I rush to the computer and place the device next to the hard drive. The magnet immediately attaches to the metal box. "Work, please work," I whisper.

Several seconds later, the video footage flickers and disappears. The entire screen turns grainy for several seconds. I pray under my breath. This is my only hope of getting away with all I've done. Finally, the screen turns black. I did it.

I try to pry the magnet off, but all that comes off is the plastic casing surrounding it. The magnet is too strong. I'll have to leave it and hope the police think Garret put it there.

I grab a clean section of my shirt and wipe my prints off everything I touched. When I am confident that no trace of me remains, I gently put the broken plastic device in Garret's hand.

I breathe a sigh of relief. There's no more evidence of me having been in Kora's room. All of this is going to get pinned on Garret.

Suddenly, Miles groans and begins to sit up. He looks towards Garret on the floor.

He can't catch me standing here. I have to leave right now. I slip quietly out the open door.

"What happened?" I hear him ask as I walk down the hallway towards the banquet hall. It's time to put on a show.

61

AMELIA (PAST)

The moment I saw the post for the opening weekend at the resort on Kora's social media, I knew this was my chance. All I had to do was bring Kora and Garret face to face and force him to decide who he wanted to be with. There was no way he could look me in the eyes and choose her. Deep down, I was convinced that he would come back to me. I was his family. I was his wife. When faced with an ultimatum, he would choose me. But, there were several moments during the weeks leading up to the trip when I was plagued with doubt. What if I was wrong?

I reached out to Kora and told her that I was a friend of her mom's and asked for more information about the resort. She didn't even question me. I was convinced I was going to have to explain how or where I met her mom, but she just believed me and sent me the details. It was way too easy. Within minutes, I booked and paid for a weekend getaway that I believed could save my marriage.

. . .

A FEW WEEKS LATER, Garret and I were on our way to the top of the mountain in the middle of a blizzard and I allowed myself to hope in a way I hadn't done in years. During the ride up the mountain, I desperately tried to remind him of what we once had, hoping he would remember how much he once loved me, but everything changed the moment Garret saw Kora at the resort.

I don't even think he knew for sure that it was her because she was all bundled up and her face was barely visible, but I could see it in his face. All the things he had promised me he would do, like taking the time to work on our relationship, took a backseat to his obsession. His reaction to seeing her was so visceral that I knew deep down in my gut that this was not just a mere fling for him. He loved her in a way that I'm not sure he ever loved me.

The moment his eyes landed on her, his face turned pale and I realized there was no way that I was going to win him back. I felt like I'd been sucker punched as it became evident that everything I had feared was true. He would do anything, even go as far as hiring someone to kill me to make sure he could be with her. I could see it in his eyes. I was worth less than nothing to him and I had to do something drastic to make it all stop.

THE PLAN WAS NOT to kill Kora. Scare her, maybe. Hurt her a little, probably, but I wasn't trying to send her to her grave. I just needed her to be scared enough of Garret to cut him off from her life for good. He couldn't even see her remotely as an option. I had to be his only choice.

The first thing that I had to do was find Kora's room. When I first arrived at the resort, after Miles escorted me to my room, I made my way back to the lobby. A new couple was checking in at the front desk and Miles was so busy he didn't even notice me slipping into the same hallway that I had seen Kora go down just a little while earlier. I told myself that if I got caught, I would just tell whoever caught me that I was looking for my husband. That wasn't entirely untrue; I did want to know where he was, but that just wasn't my primary purpose.

I actually found him before I figured out where Kora's room was. The idiot had wandered into an empty block of cells and had propped the door open to keep it from locking. I quickly removed the prop and allowed the door to slam shut.

I stepped into the shadows and felt a rush of joy as I watched him run to the door. It was almost intoxicating. He banged on the door incessantly, hoping someone would hear him. It served him right.

He was still banging for help when I walked away to find Kora's room, his cries dissipating the further away I got from the door. I was pretty confident that it was going to be a long time before anyone found him. It was clear that no one used this part of the hotel.

I traveled a few more dark hallways before turning down a well-lit corridor. Just after I turned the corner, a doorway opened. I hurried back into the darkness to avoid being detected and watched as Kora exited a room in the middle of the hall. I couldn't believe my luck. As soon as she was out of sight, I walked to the door and noted the room number, committing it to memory. I don't know why I had the idea to go outside right after. I was so hot from the anger, I thought the snow might help. I didn't even think to get a coat. Before long, I was barefoot in the lobby, telling Miles that I lost my shoes and husband.

As soon as I got back to the room, I took the time to plan what I was going to do to try to save my marriage, knowing the true depth of Garret's feelings for Kora. My desperation was turning into anger. I wanted her to be afraid of me. I wanted her to suffer.

62

MILES (PRESENT)

I awaken to a throbbing pain on the side of my head. My memory of what happened is distant and foggy, as if I'm trying to remember a dream. I open my eyes.

The bright light blinds my vision for several seconds. Eventually, the room becomes focused and I notice someone lying on their back a few feet from me.

I push myself up slowly and see that it's Garret. His eyes are wide open and he is staring into space. There's a large contusion on the side of his head. Blood pools around him. What happened?

I hear shuffling by the door. I look toward it and see Amelia just as she leaves the room. What is she doing here?

I sit for several minutes, trying to remember what happened. Eventually, the memory begins to come back to me. Amelia was here when I was fighting with Garret. She tried to help him by tackling me down. Is she the one who hit Garret on the head? Or did I do it?

Slowly, I stand, but I'm unsteady on my feet. I brace against the wall and take several deep breaths as I allow my head to stop spinning. I have a monstrous headache.

As I'm steadying myself, I remember more about the moments before I blacked out. Garret was on top of me, punching me in the face. He must have knocked me out.

I wonder what Amelia and Garret were doing back here. Why would Amelia come back to the room she was held captive in without bringing a crowd with her to witness what I had done to her?

Looking around the room, I scan for clues that could give me an idea of what happened. I notice a gaping hole in the door to the security room. The keycard device has been pried off and broken bits of it mixed with wood are scattered all around the floor. What the heck? What is going on?

I look at the computer and notice the screen is dark. I think I remember it being on before everything went black, but my memories are disjointed and spotty. They come back in short bursts as I close my eyes and force myself to think.

I remember walking back into the security room to check on Amelia in the closet, only to find the closet door busted open. That door was locked and hard to break down — or so I thought.

My last memory is of looking through the security footage, trying to find evidence about what happened to Kora. That's when Garret grabbed me and we started to fight. I don't remember much after that other than a vague recollection of someone standing at the computer. Was it Amelia? The memory is too foggy to be sure.

I walk over to the computer and try to turn it on. Nothing works. I look around both sides of the device and notice a black object stuck to the side of the box. I try to pry it off, but it's strong. Is this a magnet? Was this always here? I try to remove it, but it doesn't budge.

I look back at Garret's body and it dawns on me: All the evidence points to a man who is now deceased.

63

KORA (PAST)

I open my laptop and find an email from Miles at the top of my inbox.

Thanks so much for doing this, Kora. I promise you're not going to regret it, it says. *Do whatever you want with this flyer. Post it on social media, print it and hand it out to your friends. The more people that see it, the better.*

I click on the attachment. It's an advertisement for the resort.

Come live your wildest dreams by staying in a fully renovated prison! Great specials are available for opening weekend. A limited number of spaces are available, so act fast.

I laugh loudly. This is not exactly what I'd had in mind when I decided to sing professionally again, but it's a consistent paid gig for doing something that I love. And who knows? If the right people come, maybe I will be discovered and be able to do this full-time.

I open my social media account and make a post: *Hey guys, I'll be headlining at this resort. It's a pretty off-the-wall concept. Come check it out and say hi. It's bound to be a great time.*

I upload the flyer and post it. I watch for several minutes as the likes and comments start pouring in.

Is this really in a prison? Someone asks.

Yep, sure is, I reply.

Wow, wild, they respond. *Honestly, I've always wanted to know what it was like inside a jail, but I never wanted to do what it took to get there.*

Then get yourself a ticket, I reply. *I promise you won't regret it. At the very least, you know the entertainment is going to be fire.*

The comments keep coming in and I reply to as many as I can before logging off thirty minutes later. Hopefully, a few people will bite and we'll have a full house the first weekend.

I do have my reservations about this job. When I went to visit the resort the first time, it was like no time had passed between me and Miles. We used to date in college and I broke his heart when I left for L.A. If I'm being honest, it broke my heart also. I badly wanted him to fight for us and maybe come with me. Maybe I was delusional. But we're not kids anymore, so I'm hoping that we can potentially have a more mature relationship. At the very least, I hope things aren't weird between us when I get back there.

More than anything, though, I'm just excited to be pursuing my career as a singer. To leave all of this behind me and take a leap for my future.

I need a fresh start after everything with Garret. I really thought we had something, but I'm not about to destroy a marriage for a man, no matter how much I love him. If I want to keep living, I have to let go of the past and not look back, no matter how much it hurts. There's something amazing out there for me, a future I can't even imagine and it's just right around the corner. I can feel it.

64

AMELIA (PRESENT)

I stand at the front door, taking a deep breath of the cool morning air. The car is packed and everything I own now fits neatly into a few suitcases.

Garret's shadow no longer lingers over me. The weight of those old memories, of who I used to be and what I endured, feels lighter with each step I take toward the car. The person I was — the lonely wife who waited for scraps of affection — is gone. I am someone new now, someone stronger.

I glance back at the house one last time. It's strange how a place that once felt like a prison can look so small and insignificant now. There are memories here that used to haunt me, but they no longer hold any power. I don't need to run from them; I just choose not to carry them with me.

Garret is gone and with him, the chaos he created. I didn't set out to become someone who could take a life, but when the moment came, I did what had to be done. The police never questioned it. Garret had been implicated in Kora's death — cardiac arrest after being drugged — and the story made sense to everyone. I even told the authorities that Garret locked me in the closet instead of Miles. It made the self-defense angle stick.

I was arrested briefly for Garret's death, but they dismissed the charges once they saw the room I escaped from. To them, I was a survivor who acted in self-defense. The authorities let me walk free. Since I never said that Miles did anything wrong, he never got arrested, but I know he's suffering more than anyone who was there that night.

Sometime after Garret left the room on the night Kora died, I did something crazy. I grabbed a bottle of whiskey and my pepper spray and headed to Kora's room. I figured I would find Garret there. I didn't know what I would do, but I was planning on being the only one to come out of that room in one piece.

No one saw me as I made my way down the corridors to her room. The resort was eerily empty. Of course, later I would find out just how empty it was.

When I reached Kora's door, I knocked softly at first. Then, I took a deep breath and pounded.

Kora opened the door. She was visibly intoxicated, but somehow, she still looked dignified. Her eyes traced my body, and she clocked the bottle in my hand. "Are you gonna hit me with that, or are we drinking?" she asked plainly.

Something inside me melted at her voice. It was smooth, but you could hear the defeat behind her words.

I swallowed hard. "Where is he?"

"Not here," she said as she stepped out of the way and gestured for me to enter the room.

I stepped into the suite, my hands clenched into fists, trying to calm my pulse as it pounded in my ears. The room was beautiful — too beautiful for what I was about to do in there.

Kora floated across the room to a bar. She leaned against the counter with her hair spilling over her shoulder. She reached for a wine bottle and lifted it to her lips, a lazy, almost defiant gesture, watching me the whole time. I recognized the bottle as the one Garret had left our room with. I doubted it was a coincidence.

The urge to lash out was there, simmering beneath my skin, but there was something else too. The air was heavy with it. Resignation. As if we both knew the roles we were playing here, but couldn't be bothered with the show.

"So," I started, keeping my voice steady as I walked next to her, grabbed a glass, and poured a heavy shot of whiskey. "He was here."

She nodded. "I only let him in because I wanted to give him back the necklace. But I probably should have just pawned it."

I snorted.

Kora chuckled.

A few hot tears fell down my cheeks as I caught myself laughing... hard. I didn't even know why. It was funny, but it just caught me off guard. Something was releasing inside of me. I wasn't even mad at her. What was I doing here?

Kora sat at a table and gestured for me to sit in the chair across from her. I grabbed my whiskey and glass and obliged.

"I'm sorry. I don't even really know what I'm doing here," I said dryly, swirling my drink. I brought the glass to my lips, savoring the sharp burn as it went down. "And yet, here I am. Watching you drink wine from the bottle he probably paid for."

She took another sip. "Believe me, he owes me a lot more than this."

"I suppose he does," I said.

"Not anything like what he owes you. I am so sorry."

I nodded, but didn't speak. I wanted her to continue.

"For what it's worth," she started, "I didn't know about you at first. But I should have stopped it when I did. That was not right..."

Kora continued, so I decided to listen. I sat there and listened to the story of how they met, their love affair and the end of it. According to Kora, she broke things off because he seemed like he was going to become dangerous to me. Everything started to become clear. Kora was innocent.

I studied her, trying to see what he saw in her. She was beautiful, yes, but it was her posture that got me — so unaffected, so done with all of this.

Kora lifted the bottle. "Cheers, to our shared taste in men... and jewelry."

I laughed, and we clinked our glasses. Kora polished off her bottle. I probably could have left, but I didn't. I could have looked for Garret, but I didn't want to. I continued to drink and listen to Kora's stories. She talked to me about how she got the gig at the resort and how she was hoping to reignite a relationship from her past.

Kora's speech became slower, but I couldn't tell if it was just me who was the drunk one. She was so poised. "I should have never moved to L.A.," she said.

"Why?"

"Performing in front of large crowds is a rush, but being loved by the right person... that's something totally different."

I took a breath.

"Oh, I'm not talking about Garret. I mean, the guy I left back at home."

"Right. Yeah, I know that. But you were brave. That means something. I've never been brave." I wanted to tell her about me, but I stopped myself. I was getting caught up. I could see how everyone fell for her. It was so easy to be around her.

Kora stood up from her chair and walked to the middle of the room. She slowly laid herself down on the floor and pretended to make snow angels.

I laughed. "You are irritatingly cute," I said.

Kora laughed. "You should try it."

"To be cute?"

"No, you're already cute. Make angels with me. It'll make you happier."

"Do you just do stuff like this?"

"Only if I'm wasted," she said. "Come on, you don't even have to be in the wet and cold snow."

I stood and walked to Kora. I looked down at her face, upside-down from mine. "Okay," I said. I took my time and slowly sprawled down in the opposite direction of her, the top of my head touching her soft curls. I made a snowless angel and I cried, yet somehow, I was happy. Kora was right. Or maybe I was just drunk. After a few moments, I emotionally gathered myself and realized that she hadn't been talking.

"Kora, what was the guy's name? The one that you left behind?"

Kora didn't answer.

"Kora?" I sat up to see her out cold. I smiled sadly and thought about how we both came up short. In another life, we could have been best friends. For the first time, I didn't feel alone in this. Kora had the right idea though, by closing her eyes. I could start to feel myself get the spins and knew I was going to pass out soon as well. I slowly stood up and left the room.

I WAS SHOCKED when Miles announced that Kora was dead. When the other guests were accusing Garret of killing her, it didn't take me long to piece together what he did. It hit even harder when I realized that the last words she spoke were probably to me. It was all right there, but didn't crystallize until Garret confessed to me: when I was snooping through his stuff, there was a syringe deep in Garret's bag, the bag that he was worried about losing. I thought about the fact that he brought his *new painkillers* — ones that I'd never heard anything about. When I thought about how he left the bottle of wine in Kora's room, the picture was clear. He either poisoned her, spiked the wine, or both. The autopsy report confirmed this to be the case. Garret killed her.

His motive was simple as well. Kora knew that he wanted to hurt me, so she was a liability. That's the whole reason Garret agreed to the trip. He could get rid of her and feign ignorance about her being there in the first place; it was my idea, after all. I don't know how well he thought out the plan, but certainly, it was just a matter of time until I was next to join Kora.

Once everything was cleared, it was time for me to try to move on. I hope Miles can too. After I saw the picture of him and Kora, I knew he was the guy she was talking about. Garret did so much damage.

As for me, I've packed up my life, leaving behind the woman who was afraid to live on her own terms. I managed to land a job doing IT security for a small start-up. It's not glamorous and I'm starting from the bottom again, but I don't care. I'll climb my way back up. This time, I'm building a life on my own terms — not waiting for anyone else to give me permission or validation. Kora would approve.

I toss my bags into the backseat, feeling the thrill of possibility surge through me. For the first time in a long time, I'm not afraid of what lies ahead. My dreams are mine now and I'll make them come true on my own. Or maybe I'll get a chance and find someone to share them with, but if I don't, that'll be okay, too.

ALSO BY WINTER K. WILLIS

THE WIFE INSIDE

HOW THE AFFAIR ENDS

BEHIND THE NEIGHBOR'S DOOR

THE PERFECT GIFT

THE PERFECT EX-WIFE

THE ASSISTANT

A LETTER FROM WINTER

Dear Readers,

We hope you loved *The Last Chance* and if you did, we would be very grateful if you wrote a review. Reviews help us to reach more readers and continue to write books for you. Follow us on our Amazon page and all our socials, as well. We love connecting with our readers!

At our website below, you can sign up for our newsletter. It will keep you updated on our latest releases. Your info will never be shared and you can unsubscribe at any time.

https://www.winterkwillis.com

Thanks!
Winter

CONNECT WITH WINTER

Winter K. Willis is a pseudonym for our two-person writing team. We like to think of it as our band name. We love telling our character's stories and hope that you enjoy reading them.

Website: www.winterkwillis.com
BookBub: www.bookbub.com/authors/winter-k-willis
Instagram: www.instagram.com/winterkwillis
Facebook: https://www.facebook.com/winterkwillis

Made in the USA
Las Vegas, NV
06 February 2025

17603246R00164